YOUR FATHERS,
WHERE ARE THEY?
AND THE PROPHETS,
DO THEY LIVE
FOREVER?

YOUR FATHERS, WHERE ARE THEY? AND THE PROPHETS, DO THEY LIVE FOREVER?

A NOVEL

DAVE EGGERS

ALFRED A. KNOPF · MCSWEENEY'S BOOKS · 2014

PUBLISHED BY

ALFRED A. KNOPF

& ALFRED A. KNOPF CANADA

PUBLISHED BY

MCSWEENEY'S BOOKS

SAN FRANCISCO

THIS IS A BORZOI BOOK

Copyright © 2014 by Dave Eggers

All rights reserved. Published in the United States by Alfred A. Knopf, a division of
Random House LLC, New York, and in Canada by Alfred A. Knopf Canada, a division of
Random House of Canada Limited, Toronto, Penguin Random House companies.

www.aaknopf.com
www.randomhouse.ca
www.mcsweeneys.net

Knopf, Borzoi Books, and the colophon are registered trademarks of
Random House LLC.
Knopf Canada and colophon are trademarks.
McSweeney's and colophon are registered trademarks of McSweeney's,
a privately held company with wildly fluctuating resources.

*This is a work of fiction. Names, characters, places, and incidents either are the product of the
author's imagination or are used fictitiously. Any resemblance to actual persons, living or dead,
events, or locales is entirely coincidental.*

Library of Congress Cataloging-in-Publication Data
Eggers, Dave.
Your fathers, where are they? And the prophets, do they live forever? :
a novel / by Dave Eggers.—First edition.
pages   cm
"This is a Borzoi Book."
ISBN 978-1-101-87419-6   ISBN 978-0-307-94754-3 (eBook)
I. Title.
PS3605.G48Y69   2014813'.6—dc23   2014014536

Library and Archives Canada Cataloguing in Publication
Eggers, Dave, author
Your fathers, where are they? And the prophets, do they live forever? / Dave Eggers.
Issued in print and electronic formats.
ISBN 978-0-345-80959-9   ISBN 978-0-345-80961-2 (eBook)
I. Title.
PS3605.G34Y69   2014 813'.6   C2014-902193-3

Jacket design by T. S. Hawkins and Stephanie Ross

Manufactured in the United States of America
First Edition

JUN - - 2014

YOUR FATHERS,
WHERE ARE THEY?
AND THE PROPHETS,
DO THEY LIVE
FOREVER?

BUILDING 52

—I did it. You're really here. An astronaut. Jesus.

   —Who's that?

   —You probably have a headache. From the chloroform.

   —What? Where am I? Where is this place? Who the fuck are you?

   —You don't recognize me?

   —What? No. What is this?

   —That? It's a chain. It's attached to that post. Don't pull on it.

   —Holy shit. Holy shit.

   —I said don't pull on it. And I have to tell you right away how sorry I am that you're here under these circumstances.

   —Who are you?

   —We know each other, Kev. From way back. And I didn't want to bring you here like this. I mean, I'd rather just grab a beer with you sometime, but you didn't answer any of my letters and then I saw you were coming through town so— Really, don't yank on that. You'll mess up your leg.

—Why the fuck am I here?

—You're here because I brought you here.

—You did this? You have me chained to a post?

—Isn't that thing great? I don't know if you'd call it a post. Whatever it is, it's incredibly strong. This place came with them. This was a military base, so there are these weird fixtures here and there. That thing you're chained to can hold ten thousand pounds, and just about every building here has one. Stop pulling on it.

—Help!

—Don't yell. There's no one for miles. And the ocean's just over the hill, so between the waves and the wind you'd barely hear a cannon fire from here. But they're not firing cannons anymore.

—Help!

—Jesus. Stop. That's way too loud. This is all cement, man. Hear that echo?

—Help! Help!

—I figured you might yell, so if it's going to be now, just tell me. I can't stay here while you do that.

—Help!

—My respect for you is plummeting.

—Help! Help! Help! Hello—

—All right. Jesus Christ. I'll be back when you're done.

•

4

—You done?

—Fuck you.

—You know, I've never heard you swear before. That's one of the main things I remember about you, that you never swore. You were such a serious guy, so precise and careful and upstanding. And with the crew cut and those short-sleeve button-downs, you were such a throwback. I guess you have to be if you want to be an astronaut— you have to be that kind of tidy. Have that kind of purity.

—I don't know you.

—What? Yes you do. You don't remember?

—No. I don't know anyone like you.

—Stop. Just think about it. Who am I?

—No.

—You're chained to a post. You might as well guess. How do we know each other?

—Fuck you.

—No.

—Help!

—Don't. Can't you hear how loud it is in here? You hear the echo?

—Help! Help!

—I'm so disappointed in you, Kev.

—Help! Help! Help!

—Okay. I'm leaving till you get your shit together.

•

—Now are you done? It's cold out there at night. The wind comes up the bluff and the Pacific— I don't know. It gets bitter. With the sun out it's almost balmy, but when it drops it gets arctic quick. You must be hoarse. You want some water?

—

—I'll just leave this bottle here. Drink it when you want. That's why I left your left hand free. We'll be here awhile, so just know I'll make sure you eat and have whatever else you need. I have some blankets in the van, too.

—How'd you get me here? Were you the guy moving that couch?

—That was me. I saw that trick in a movie. I can't believe it worked. You helped me move the couch into the van, and I tased you, then I used some chloroform and drove you here. You want to hear the whole thing? It's pretty incredible.

—No.

—You can't really park very close to this building we're in, so I dragged you out of the van onto that cart there—you can see it outside. It was already here, and it works perfectly. I could push an elephant on that thing. So I got you onto that cart, then I pulled you a quarter mile from the parking lot to this building. To be honest, I'm still just dazed thinking that all this worked. You've got me by, what, thirty pounds, and you're definitely in better shape than I could ever be. But still it worked. You're a fucking astronaut and now I have you here. This is a great day.

—You're nuts.

—No, no. I'm not. First of all, I'm sorry. I never thought I'd do something like this, but everything lately made it necessary. I've never hurt anyone in my life, and I won't hurt you. I would never harm you, Kev. I want you to understand that. So you don't need to struggle or anything. I'll let you go tomorrow after we talk for a while.

—You're really fucking nuts.

—I'm really not. Really. I want you to stop saying that, because I'm not. I'm a moral man and I'm a principled man.

—Fuck you.

—Stop saying that, too. I don't like you when you swear. Let's get back to remembering me. Do you?

—No.

—Kev, stop. Just look at me. The sooner we get through all this, the sooner I can let you go.

—You let me go and I'll kill you.

—Hey. Hey. Why would you *say* that? That doesn't make any sense. You just set yourself back *hours*. Maybe more. I was planning to let you go later on tonight. Maybe tomorrow at the latest. But now you've got me scared. I didn't picture you as a violent type. Jesus, Kev, you're an astronaut! You shouldn't be going around threatening people.

—You've got me chained to a post.

—Still. What I did to you was methodical and nonviolent. It was a means to an end. I wanted to talk to you, and you haven't answered my letters, so I didn't think I had a choice. I really do apologize for having to do it this way. I've been in a strange place lately. I was getting these migraines, I couldn't sleep. Holy shit, the pressure! The questions were piling up and were strangling me at night. Have you ever had that, where you're lying there, and the questions are just these asps wrapping themselves around your throat?

—You are so fucking nuts.

—You know what, Kev? I'm not. But I have to say, right when I said *asps* I knew it was a mistake. Someone like you hears that word, the specificity of it, and you think I'm some obsessive weirdo.

—But you're not.

—See, the sarcasm, too. That's new. I remember you being so sincere. I privately admired that. I don't like this new edge. Now listen, I think you can tell I have my faculties together.

—Even though you kidnapped me and brought me here.

—Exactly *because* I brought you here—successfully. I made a plan, executed it, and I brought an astronaut to an abandoned military base one hundred and ten miles away from where I abducted you. That makes me a pretty competent person, correct?

—

—Kev. You work for the government, right?

—I work for NASA.

—Which is a government agency. And every day the government is bringing some enemy combatant to some undisclosed location to interrogate them, right? So what's wrong with me doing the same thing?

—So I'm an enemy combatant.

—No. Maybe that was a poor comparison.

—Buddy, you'll be in prison the rest of your life.

—I don't think so. Only dumb people get caught.

—And you're a brilliant criminal mastermind.

—No. No, Kev. I've never done anything illegal in my life. Isn't that amazing? I really haven't. The great crimes are committed by first-timers. I see you looking around. Isn't this place great? How cool is it that we're actually on a military base? You recognize this stuff? Look around. This was some kind of artillery storage building. I think they would fasten the cannons or whatever to these posts so they could move back and forth to absorb the kickback. I'm not really sure, but why else would they have these posts here?

—I'm going to fucking kill you. But the cops will kill you first.

—Kev, that won't happen.

—You don't think there's a massive manhunt to find out what happened to me?

—Don't be conceited. You were never conceited. You were one of those guys who knows he's smart and strong and destined for great things, but you also knew it wasn't going to help you if you advertised it to the world. So you had a nice kind of public humility thing working for you. I liked that. I understood your whole gambit, but I liked it and respected it. So don't blow it with the "I'm an astronaut" bravado.

—Fine. But you're still dead. They'll find me in twenty-four hours.

—No, they won't. I texted three people from your phone, telling them all you were in different places. I told one of your NASA coworkers you had a death in the family. And I told your parents you were on a training assignment. Thank god for texting—I can impersonate you perfectly. Then I turned your phone off and threw it away.

—There's a hundred things you haven't thought of.

—Maybe. Maybe not. So are you wondering where you are? This whole base is decommissioned and falling apart. No one knows what to do with it, so it's just standing here, rotting on billion-dollar land. You can't see it from here, but the ocean is about a half mile down the slope. The views are incredible. But on this land there are just these crumbling old buildings. There are hundreds of them, and twenty more like this one, all in a row. I think this one was used to test chemical weapons. There's one nearby where they taught interrogation methods. And the ones like this, they all have these posts you can hook things onto. Why are you looking at me like that? Does that mean you recognize me?

—No.

—Yes you do.

—I don't. You're a fucking lunatic and I told you, I don't know lunatics. My life's been charmed that way.

—Kev. I really want to get started. So we're either going to get started the way I hope we can get started, with us talking, or I'll tase you, get you in line a bit, and then we'll get started. So why not just talk to me? Let's go about this like men. We have a task ahead of us and we might as well do it. You were always all business, getting things taken care of, moving on. I expect that kind of efficiency from you. Now where am I from? How do you know me?

—I don't know. I've never been to prison. I'm assuming you escaped from somewhere.

—Kev, you see that taser there? If you decide not to talk with me then I tase you. If you yell for help, I leave the building till you shut up, then I come back and tase you. It's so much better if we just talk.

—And then what? You kill me.

—I couldn't kill you. I've never killed anything.

—But if I tell anyone about this, you're in prison for ten, twenty years. Kidnapping an astronaut?

—That's my problem, not yours. Obviously, you're locked to a post, so I have the upper hand in terms of *when* someone finds you and how far away I can be by the time you're found. Kev, I don't mean to be a dick, but can we get started? Obviously I have this whole thing figured out. I brought you this far, and I managed to get you chained up. I mean, I'm not an idiot. I've been planning this for a while. So can we start?

—And if I talk to you then you let me go?

—I won't harm you. You'll be rescued eventually. I leave, I send a message to someone, telling them where you are, and they come to find you. By then I'm on my way. So one more time before I get angry. How do we know each other?

—College.

—Ah. There you go. College. You remember my name?

—No.

—Kev, c'mon.

—I don't know.

—But you knew I was from college.

—I didn't know that. I guessed.

—C'mon. Think.

—Bob?

—You know my name isn't Bob. No one's name is Bob.

—Dick?

—Dick? Oh, I get it. That's a name you're calling me. Listen. I want to think you're a nice guy, so just tell me you remember my name.

—Okay. I remember you.

—Good. And my name is . . .

—Steve.

—No.

—Bob.

—Bob again? Really?

—Rob? Danny?

—You really don't know! Okay, let's walk through it, slowly. Was I from undergrad or grad school?

—Undergrad.

—Thank you. I was three years younger. Ring a bell?

—No.

—Think Intro to Aerospace Engineering. You were a TA.

—There were a hundred and twenty kids in that class.

—But think. I stayed after a lot. I asked you questions about time travel.

—You used to wear Timberlands?

—Aha. There you go. And my name is . . .

—Gus.

—Close! Thomas.

—Thomas? Sure, I remember. I could never forget you. So Thomas, why the fuck do you have me chained to a post?

—Kev, did you know Neil Armstrong died today?

—Yes, I did know that.

—How did that affect you?

—How did that affect me?

—Yes, how did that affect you?

—I don't know. I was sad. He was a great man.

—He went to the moon.

—Yes he did.

12

—But you won't go to the moon.

—No. Why would I go to the moon?

—Because you're an astronaut.

—Astronauts don't go to the moon.

—They don't anymore.

—No.

—Right. And how do you feel about that, Kev?

—Jesus Christ.

—I have a taser, Kev. You're better off answering.

—I didn't care about going to the moon. It hasn't been a NASA priority for forty years.

—You wanted to be on the Shuttle.

—Yes.

—I bet you wonder how I knew that.

—No, I don't.

—You're not curious?

—Every astronaut wanted to go on the Shuttle.

—Sure, but I know how long you've wanted it. You told me one day you were going to go up in the Shuttle. Remember that?

—No.

—You probably said that a lot. But I remember it so well. It was so steady, you were so sure. You inspired me. You asked me what I wanted to do with my life. I think you asked me just so you could answer the question yourself. So I said something about being a cop or FBI agent or something, and do you remember what you said? This was right outside Moore Hall. It was a crisp fall day.

—I said I wanted to go up in the Shuttle.

—Exactly! Do you really remember, or are you just humoring me?

—I don't know.

—Kev, you really better take this seriously. I take this seriously. I went through a fuckload of trouble to get you here, so you must know I'm serious. Now with all fucking seriousness, do you remember that day when you looked me in the eye and told me you were absolutely sure you would go up in the Shuttle?

—Yes. I do.

—Good. And now where are you?

—I'm in a military base chained to a post.

—Good. Good one. But you know what I mean. I mean, where are you in your life now? You're sure as hell not on the Shuttle.

—The Shuttle is decommissioned.

—Right. A year after you became an astronaut.

—You know too much about me.

—Of course I know about you! We all did. You became an astronaut! You actually did it. You didn't know how much people were paying attention, did you, Kev? That little college we went to, with what, five thousand people, most of them idiots except you and me? And you end up going to MIT, get your master's in aerospace engineering, and you're in the Navy, too? I mean, you were my fucking hero, man. Everything you said you were going to do, you did. It was incredible. You were the one fulfilled promise I've ever known in this life. You know how rarely a promise is kept? A kept promise is like a white whale, man! But when you became an astronaut you kept a promise, a big fucking promise, and I felt like from there any promise could be kept. That all promises could be kept—should be kept.

—I'm glad you feel that way.

—But then they pulled the Shuttle from you. And I thought,

Ah, there it is again. The bait and switch. The inevitable collapse of anything seeming solid. The breaking of every last goddamned promise on Earth. But for a while there you were a god. You promised you'd become an astronaut and you became one. Just one thing after another, except that one year, which I'll ask you about later. I know a few things about that one year.

—Jesus Christ. You know, I keep thinking I'll wake up. I mean, I know this is a nightmare, but it's one of those ones where you can't wake up.

—Kev, you talking to yourself now?

—Go fuck yourself.

—Kev, I'm really serious about the swearing. Stop it. I don't like it from you. I really don't, and I won't accept it. I will actually do what I can to stop you from cursing more.

—Fuck you.

—Kev. Last warning. I honestly mean it. You must know by now I'm a man of some resolve. When I determine to do something, I do it, just like you. I brought you here, and I have a taser here, and I'm sure I can find some other tools around that will be unpleasant. And the fact that I've never done anything violent in my life will not be good for you. It'll make me messy, and I'll make mistakes that a more experienced person would not.

—You say you'll release me tonight?

—I'll let you go as soon as I can. As soon as I'm satisfied.

—Okay. Let's do it then.

—Really?

—Yup. Let's start.

—Good. You know I'm a moral man.

—Of course you are.

—I am. I'm a man of principle, just like you.

—Right.

—Good. You know, now, finally, *finally,* I'm seeing the exact guy who got through MIT and the Navy and all these academies and became an astronaut. This is how you did it. You set a goal and you accomplished it. And this is just like that. I gave you the parameters and now you'll work within them, execute the plan, and move on to the next step. I love that about you. You're *still* my hero.

—I'm glad. Let's do it then.

—But don't be overanxious. This has to unfold naturally. I don't want it to be perfunctory.

—Right.

—Your answers have to be truthful. The questions might even hurt. If I think you're doing some political non-answer kind of bullshit, you will stay here till I get some straight, maybe even painful answers, okay?

—I understand.

—Okay, good. So we're going to go through things for a few minutes. I've read about your path but I need to hear it from you. You ready?

—Yes.

—You were on the baseball team all four years in college, and you still got a 4.0. Is that correct?

—Yes.

—How the hell did you do that?

—I didn't go out. I went to college to study and get to the next step.

—When did you know what the next step was?

—Before I started college.

—So before you started college, you knew what you would do after?

—Of course.

—What do you mean, of course? No one thinks that way.

—A lot of people do. I had to. The second I got to college, twenty thousand others who wanted to be astronauts were already ahead of me.

—How?

—Maybe they went to a better college. Maybe they were part of a demographic NASA didn't have well represented. Maybe they didn't have asthma when they were kids. Maybe they had better connections.

—Did you really have asthma?

—Until I was twelve.

—Then what?

—Then I didn't.

—I didn't know that was possible.

—It is.

—You had totally diagnosed asthma with an inhaler and everything?

—Yes.

—And then no more inhaler, no asthma?

—None.

—See, you are a *god*! I *love* that.

—It happens sometimes. Many young people see their symptoms disappear with dietary changes or a change of climate.

—And now you're talking like an astronaut again. Thank you.

"Young people, dietary changes." That's what an astronaut would say. He wouldn't say "kids," and he would do what you did, which was turn your own story into something about the Youth of America. I love that. You are good. Did they give you special PR training at NASA?

—I haven't gotten that far.

—Okay wait. Hold that thought. We'll get there. But first I want to back up. We're gonna talk about the steps. You knew you were in undergrad to get your engineering degree. Was it in— What kind of engineering was it in?

—Aerospace engineering.

—And you're somehow a catcher on the baseball team. How the hell did that happen?

—I played in high school, and walked on the team.

—So you weren't on a scholarship?

—I was on a partial academic scholarship.

—No!

—Yes.

—See, I'm so glad we did this. I'm so glad I brought you here, because already my faith in humanity has been partially restored. Here you were on the baseball team, and all this time I figured you were in college on a baseball scholarship, and that's why you played four years while your real priority was grades and getting to the next step. But now I find out that the catcher for the fucking baseball team was on an academic scholarship! That is perfect. That is astounding.

—Well, I wasn't good enough to get a full ride with baseball.

—But you *played*! I watched you play. You started our senior year, when the other guy, what's his name . . .

—Julian Gonzalez.

—Right, when he transferred, you played every game. And you still kept a 4.0. I mean, did the rest of the team think you were some kind of freak?

—They did.

—Why, because you didn't go out at night, screw girls and all that?

—Basically.

—But then you *did* screw a girl!

—What?

—Oh shit. Sorry. I didn't mean to jump into this. But I know about Jennifer and the, you know.

—What?

—We'll get to that later.

—Fuck you.

—I told you it might get uncomfortable.

—I'm done with this.

—Okay listen. I'm sorry. We were really cooking there. Please, I won't bring up Jennifer. I already know about all that anyway. I asked around and I think I got the story.

—You got what story, asshole?

—Don't fuck with me, Kev! You did two things wrong just now. You threatened me and you swore again.

—I didn't threaten you, but I will. I will fucking tear your head off.

—See, this is such a disappointment. Is that what held you back—your temper? Don't pull on that chain.

—I get mad when people chain me up and ask me about my girlfriend from a hundred years ago.

—I bet you get mad a lot. Especially now. Yeah, you have a lot to be mad about now. And I do, too. That's fine. That's understandable. See, that's another way we're similar. We both execute our plans, and we both have heavy gears turning in our heads that threaten to crush our skulls.

—Oh god, you're so nuts! Holy shit.

—If you say that again, I'm tasing you, Kev. Not because I want to, but because you calling me nuts is so expected and so boring. Call the kidnapper nuts, blah blah, it's boring. You've called me nuts twenty times and it hasn't improved your situation. And I'm getting tired of your distractions. I just want to get through this without hurting you, okay?

—

—Okay, now back to the narrative. After college there was that lost year, and then you went to MIT. Was that the same thing, where you knew what you were there to do?

—I was getting a master's in aerospace engineering. Of course I knew what I was there to do. I wasn't getting some degree in basket making.

—Okay, fine. So MIT was what, two years?

—Three.

—Wow, you're already in school for seven years. You know what I was doing after undergrad?

—No.

—My uncle made me work in his factory. Can you imagine that? I had a college degree and he made me work on the floor, next to a bunch of Eastern European women. How fucked up is that?

—I don't know, Don.

—Thomas.

—Sorry. Thomas.

—Wait. You remember my friend Don?

—No.

—I think you might. That is so weird that you said Don. Don was your biggest fan. You remember him? He was usually with me. He went to the same school as you and me.

—I don't remember him.

—For a couple years at least. He was Vietnamese American? Really good-looking guy?

—I don't know, Thomas. It's been a long time.

—But he was always with me. There's a reason you just mentioned his name. That can't be a coincidence.

—I think it was a coincidence. I'm sorry.

—Jesus, that is weird. Don's been on my mind all the time lately. You know he died?

—No, I didn't. I didn't know Don. But I'm sorry he died.

—It was a while ago now. God, two years or so. This is so eerie, because I swear Don really admired you. I mean, he had more of a NASA jones than even I did. He asked about you a lot in school, after I found out you were trying to get on the Shuttle. He asked about you after school, too. It was more him, actually, who kept reminding me about you. It was one of the things we always talked about. He knew when you joined the Navy. I'd call or he'd call and we'd talk and pretty soon one of us would say, Hey, how's Kev Paciorek doing? You know, just a check-in. I think he would have loved to be an astronaut himself. But who ever heard of a Vietnamese-American astronaut, right?

—There are Asian-American astronauts.

—But back then, none, right? No one who looked like Don. And he didn't have the most stable home life. I think you have to be from some kind of solid family unit, right?

—My parents were divorced.

—Oh yeah. I knew that.

—Listen, I'm sorry I mentioned his name. It was an accident. I'm really sorry he died so young.

—That's okay. Yeah. I mean, that's fine. But I'm convinced there's a reason. You don't remember his face? He had these dark eyes, this big white smile? God, this is weird. I'm . . . I'm just going outside for a second.

•

—Sorry about that. Crap is it cold out there. It's the wind off the ocean that gets you. And the lack of humidity. There's nothing to the air here, nothing held in it, no heat or water or weight. It's just this set of steel blades that churns over the ocean and up the bluffs and across these hills. It was different where you grew up, right Kev? I mean, there was humidity there. You didn't have to rush to get your winter coat the second the sun dropped.

—So I take it you live around here?

—I can't really talk about where I live, can I, Kev? We should really get back to your story. Sorry I had to take a walk. I just needed some time to figure some things out, and I think I did. So you were saying that after MIT, what?

—I joined the Navy.

—As what?

—As an ensign.

—Where was this?

—Pensacola.

—Were you flying planes or what?

—Yes, I was reporting to the Naval Air Training Command.

—But you flew, right?

—A few years later I went to Test Pilot School at Patuxent River.

—That's in Maryland. Right. I knew that. So you were testing planes then? Flying?

—I was flying F-18s and KC-130s.

—Those are what, fighter jets?

—Yes, the F-18 is a twin-engine tactical aircraft. A KC-130 is a tanker that provides in-flight refueling.

—You sound like yourself again. All that jargon spewed out so fluidly and confidently. You never had doubts about yourself, or any of these numbers or theories or equations. That was how you were as a TA, too. You remember the professor in that class?

—Schmidt.

—Right. Remember he used to jog to class? He'd be wearing a sweatsuit to class, and he'd stand up there, meandering all over the place. I think he'd had a lot of trouble in his life, right?

—I don't know.

—So that's a yes. And he went through the material pretty well, but he seemed to question the point of it all. I don't think he liked academia. He wasn't doing any significant research, was he?

—The man is dead. I don't know the point in questioning his state of mind during that class.

—I think he was really sad. He talked about losing his wife, as if she'd been taken away from him by some shadowy army that should be held accountable. But it was cancer, right?

—I believe so.

—But she must have been sixty, like him, right? You hit sixty and all bets are off. Wait, weren't you stationed in Pakistan for a while?

—After Monterey. I went to the Defense Language Institute for a while.

—For what? Arabic?

—Urdu.

—So you speak Urdu.

—I do. Not as well as I used to.

—See, this bends my mind. Catcher on the baseball team, 4.0. MIT for engineering. Then you speak Urdu and become an astronaut with NASA. And now it's defunded.

—It's not defunded. The funding is going elsewhere.

—Into little robots. WALL-Es that putter around Mars.

—There's real value to that.

—Kev, c'mon. You know you're pissed.

—I'm not pissed. I knew what I was getting into.

—Did you? You really thought that in 1998, when you said you wanted to go up in the Shuttle, that the whole program would be killed twelve years later? That they'd be parading the shuttles around the country like some kind of dead animal?

—People liked that.

—It was sick. Instead of the Shuttle actually flying anywhere, they flew it around on top of a 747. It was a joke. Just to send home the point that the whole thing's defunct, that our greatest engineering triumph needs to go piggyback on some other plane. It was pathetic.

—It was just a show, Thomas. Nothing to get upset about.

—Well, I am upset. Why aren't we on the moon now?

—As we speak?

—What happened to a colony on the moon? You know it's possible. I heard you talk about it in some interview.

—Well, it is possible. But it costs a lot of money, and we don't have that money.

—Of course we do.

—Who says?

—We have the money.

—How do we have the money?

—We just spent five trillion dollars on useless wars. That could have gone to the moon. Or Mars. Or the Shuttle. Or something that would inspire us in some goddamned way. How long has it been since we did any one fucking thing that inspired anyone?

—We elected a black president.

—Fine. That was good. But as a nation, as a fucking world? When did we do anything remotely like the Shuttle, or Apollo?

—The Space Station.

—The International Space Station? Are you kidding? I never liked that thing. Floating up there helpless like some space kite.

—Then you don't know what you're talking about. A lot of very useful data has come out of the ISS.

—I know you have to toe the party line there. That's fine. We both know it's bullshit. The ISS sucks and you know it. It's a box kite in space. So that's where you're headed now? I heard about that. Is that where you're going?

—That's my best bet now.

—But you have to get on a Russian rocket to get there.

—Seems that way.

—Now we have to buy seats on Russian rockets! How fucked up is that? Can you imagine? What kind of inverted fucked-up world, right? We start the space race because the Russians strike first with Sputnik. The competition drives the entire process for a decade. We get to the moon first, then we go back again and again, and we keep innovating, reaching, and it's beautiful, right? It coincides directly with the best years of the last fifty.

—I don't know about that.

—Well, whatever. It worked. And now we kill it all, and we pay the Russians for a backseat on their rockets. You couldn't write a sicker ending to the whole story. How do the Russians have money for rockets and we don't?

—They've prioritized differently.

—They've prioritized correctly.

—What do you want me to say?

—I want you to be pissed.

—I can't do anything about it. And I'm not about to trash NASA for you, chained up like this.

—I don't expect you to trash NASA. But look at us, on this vast land worth a billion dollars. You can't see it, but the views here are incredible. This is thirty thousand acres on the Pacific coast. You sell some of this land and we could pay for a lunar colony.

—You couldn't buy an outhouse on the moon.

—But you could get a start.

—Not likely.

—You know what? Hold on a second. What time is it?

—

—I guess it's hard for you to check. I think I have time. I have an idea. Hold on a sec. Actually, you'll have to hold on a while. Maybe seven hours or so. I think I can do this. And here's some food. It's all I brought. And some milk. You like milk?

—Where are you going?

—I know you like milk. You drank it in class. You remember? Jesus, you were so pure, like some fucking unicorn.

—Where are you going?

—I have an idea. You gave me an idea.

BUILDING 53

—First of all, sir, I want to apologize. I didn't want to bring you here,
but I really couldn't think of any way around it.

   —Who are you?

   —We've met once, but I don't know if you'd remember. But it
doesn't matter so much who I am. I just want to apologize for bringing you here. I didn't have any intention of doing this, but then
circumstances conspired to make it necessary. I have this astronaut
next door, and he was talking about what happened to him and the
Shuttle, and we were talking about the moon, and colonies there, and
about government priorities, and then I had this idea that someone
like you would have some of the answers that we needed. And I knew
you'd retired out this way, so I had to go and get you and bring
you here.

   —Holy Christ on a cracker.

—Again, I'm really sorry.

—You planning to harm me?

—I'm glad you asked that, sir. The good news is I'm not planning to harm you. The shackles are just a formality. It's not like I think you're dangerous or anything, given your disability. But I had to shackle the astronaut, because he could kill me if he wanted to, and then it seemed like the safest bet to shackle you, too, and the posts are here in every building, and I had a boxful of handcuffs, so it was all pretty convenient.

—I don't understand any of this.

—Well, the chloroform will keep your head a little cloudy for a while. But I just want to say I'm very honored to have you here. I respect your service to the country, both as a soldier and as a congressman. That's why I gave you the couch. There are couches all over the place out here, just dumped in the street like the place got looted. Is it comfortable enough?

—How the hell did you get me here?

—Sir, I don't mean any disrespect to you, but a man your age, and with your, you know, missing limbs, you were a lot easier than the astronaut.

—Wait, what, son? You have an astronaut out here?

—Yes sir. I mentioned that before. He's fine. I haven't harmed the astronaut and I won't harm you.

—Kid, you look like a pretty clean-cut guy. Do you have any idea how serious this is?

—I do, sir. I really do. I don't take it lightly. But like I said, I didn't think I had much choice but to bring the astronaut here, and when I was talking to him, all these questions came up and so many of them had answers only someone like you could provide.

—How's that, son? Questions?

—Well, as a congressman . . .

—I'm no longer in office, you realize.

—I know that, sir. But you were in office a good long while, and I'm sure that you've had expertise with some of the questions I have.

—And you brought me out here to answer them? You ever hear of a telephone or e-mail or whatnot?

—Well, sure, but that might have taken a long time. And after I took the astronaut, I figured I only have a certain window before I'm caught or found or something else happens to me, so I thought I might as well get it all figured out in one fell swoop.

—And why me again?

—Yes, sir, that's a fair question. But again, once the astronaut and I started talking, in the back of my mind I thought, Well, I bet Congressman Dickinson would have something to say about this. I knew you'd retired around here, and given you're retired, I figured you wouldn't have a security detail anymore.

—So you could kidnap me.

—Well, yes. Again, I'm so sorry. I really don't like the word *kidnap*.

—You were the guy who came to the house to rewire the phones?

—Yeah, I just needed a way into the house, and, you know, it worked. I figured it might not be very difficult, given you're in a wheelchair. I was hoping no one else was home. I waited a bit until— Was that your daughter?

—My wife.

—Oh, sorry. She was very young. Okay, good. Congratulations. That's very good. That's nice. So I had to wait until she left. How long have you been together?

—Son, you are batshit crazy.

—I'm really not.

—Of course you are. But when you showed up that day, you looked like a nice clean-cut guy. We talked about the 49ers.

—They're really having a good year, aren't they? And I really am a clean-cut guy. I'm just stuck in a tight spot right now. These headaches are messing with my life, and the ceiling just seems to be lowering on me every day. But just yesterday, with the astronaut, I felt like I was on the verge of something. I was breathing better. And I know you'll help me even more. So can we start?

—Start what, son?

—I just have some questions. Once I ask them, you're free. Especially if you answer them honestly. And I know you will; I've admired your candor and integrity since the beginning. And again, I'm very humbled by your service to this country. I know it must have been quite a sacrifice to lose two limbs in Vietnam.

—Son, I know that you're a confused young man, and I want to help you. I saw a lot of people like you back in the day, especially when I rotated back to the States, so I know where you're coming from. I really do. If anyone understands the mind of a young man whose skull is fastened one turn too tight, it's me. But I want to say for the record that I think you doing it this way is deplorable and bizarre, and you would be best off cutting your losses and calling this quits.

—Nah, I'd rather not.

—If you left right now, and told the authorities where we are, I would personally see to it that you were treated with some compassion. That you got some help.

—See, but *you're* the help I need. If you cooperate, I will be helped. I don't need medicine or therapy. I need my questions answered.

—What kind of questions, son?

—Not all that difficult. Basic stuff. You'll know the answers.

—

—So we're ready?

—Hell.

—Great.

—For the sake of getting this over with.

—Okay. Okay. My first question—and the main one—is, Why isn't my buddy Kev Paciorek in space?

—Pardon?

—He's an astronaut. The guy next door.

—You kidnapped your buddy?

—It's all worked out now. He gets it.

—What's that?

—I've known him fifteen years. We understand each other. And back when we were in college he looked me in the eye and he said, Someday I'm going up in the Shuttle. At the time, I thought, Bullshit, no way. But then he kept getting closer to it. He cleared every hurdle. He was fucking Jesus. He walked on water, water into wine, everything. He did everything they told him to. Joined the Navy. MIT, grad degrees. He speaks Urdu for fuck's sake. And all because he wanted to go up in the Shuttle or maybe to a lunar colony. And then twelve years later he becomes an astronaut, and a few months later, they kill the Shuttle, and they defund everything NASA does, and so instead he's waiting in line to maybe get a ride on some shit-ass Russian rocket to some piece-of-shit Space Station full of pussies.

—Son, did you really kidnap me to talk about the Space Shuttle?

—Mainly, yes.

—Holy Jesus.

—Kev said he was going to be an astronaut, and he did everything he was asked to do to become one. But now it means nothing. That just seems like the worst kind of thing, to tell a generation or two that the finish line is here, that the requirements to get there are this and this and this, but then, just as we get there, you move the finish line.

—Now son, just so I understand. You're saying I'm the one who did this, that I personally moved the finish line?

—I think you were in a position to hold the line.

—You do see me sitting here, do you not? Do you see a man who is missing two key limbs? Do you think a man missing two key limbs and a thumb, all of them taken in a piece-of-shit foreign war, is part of the machinery you're talking about? You think I'm the enemy?

—Well why were you in Congress if you weren't part of the machinery?

—I was in the machinery to try to *fix* that machine, you dummy! Why the hell do you think there were a half-dozen Vietnam vets on the Democrat side of things in the Senate and House? Someone had to talk some sense down there.

—How did it happen, by the way? I know I should know, but I don't.

—How did what happen?

—What happened to your leg and arm? Sorry to be indelicate.

—I don't think you're in danger of being confused with a man of delicacy or subtlety, son. Before I tell you, I should ask, did you happen to bring any of my prescriptions here? I need them for my stumps and for my arrhythmia.

—I grabbed what I could. I didn't have much time. They're in the duffel bag behind you. I also brought the bottle by your bed. Which was a surprise to me, that you have a bottle of gin by your bedside. That seemed like some kind of cliché, the aging vet drinking himself to sleep.

—Now you actually *are* being indelicate. That's really none of your goddamned business, kid. And just because there was a bottle by the bed doesn't mean this is some kind of long-standing habit or ritual.

—Fine.

—I don't know why I'm explaining myself to you.

—You're right. No need. It's not why you're here. And anyway, I understand if you need some help getting to sleep. I haven't had to go through what you did, I haven't really seen fuck-all compared to you, and I need eleven hours every night to sleep six or seven. So I would never judge.

—Thanks. That's a comfort.

—No problem.

—Son, in your head, is this what qualifies as bonding?

—See, you're being so condescending, and I didn't want you to be that way toward me. Do you think I'm somehow inferior because I wasn't part of some war? Because I wasn't drafted and grew up in peacetime and never had to struggle the way you have?

—No. I don't.

—I do.

—*You* do?

—I do. I grew up next to this base, sir, and my father was a contractor here. And I'm pretty sure that I would have turned out better, and everyone I know would have turned out better, if we'd been part of some universal struggle, some cause greater than ourselves.

—And you think Vietnam was that?

—Well, no, not necessarily.

—So what the hell are you talking about? Do you know how fucked up most of the men who came back from Vietnam are? You're damned lucky your dad didn't have to fight. You wanted to be part of that?

—No. No, not that exact conflict. But I just mean . . .

—You wish you were part of some wonderful video game conflict with a clear moral objective.

—Or something else. Something else that brought everyone together with a unity of purpose, and some sense of shared sacrifice.

—Son, judging just by the fact that you're kidnapping people and chaining them to posts, I knew you were confused. But in actuality your brain is plain scrambled. One minute you're complaining about your astronaut buddy who didn't get to ride on a cool spaceship, and the next you're saying you wish you'd been drafted. I mean, none of this squares, son. What exactly brought you to this point?

—I don't know. Actually, I think I do know. It's because nothing's happened to me. And I think that's a waste on your part. You should have found some kind of purpose for me.

—Who should have?

—The government. The state. Anyone, I don't know. Why didn't you tell me what to do? They told *you* what to do, and you went and fought and sacrificed and then came back and had a mission . . .

—Kid, do you know how I lost my limbs?

—That's why I was asking before. I assume you saved lives. You got a Bronze Star and . . .

—No. I didn't save any lives. I was eating lunch.

—What? No.

—I lost my limbs because I was eating my lunch near the wrong dipshit who hadn't secured his grenades.

—That can't be true.

—Listen. I was alone, eating my lunch. This kid had just rotated in from Mississippi, and he was some idiotic bumpkin with too much energy. He thought we were friends, so he came running toward me, pretending he was charging at me like a moose. Just some dumb thing young men do. A grenade fell off his uniform, the pin was pulled, and it rolled directly to me and landed at my feet. I just had time to turn my head away when it went off. That was the moment of unified purpose and shared sacrifice that separated me from my limbs.

—That's depressing.

—Yes, it is depressing. So when I got back I tried to talk some sense into anyone who thought going into some country on the other end of the world to exert our will would be a cute idea, and the main problem with a cute idea like that is that these plans are carried out by groups of nineteen-year-olds who can't tie their shoes and who think it's great fun to run around goofing with grenades poorly secured to their uniforms. Wars put young men in close proximity to grenades and guns and a hundred other things they will find a way to fuck up. These days men in war get themselves killed far more often than they get killed by someone else.

—I guess.

—Do you understand the difference, son?

—I think so.

—Because I look at you and wouldn't trust you with a book of matches. You've got a head full of rocks, kid. And there are a hundred thousand others like you in the desert right now, and it's no wonder they're killing civilians and raping women soldiers and shooting themselves in the leg. I don't mean to besmirch the character of these young men and women, because I know most of them are the salt of the earth, but my point is that they should be kept safe and kept out of the way of dangerous things. Young men need to be kept away from guns, bombs, women, cars, hard alcohol and heavy machinery. If I had my way they'd be cryogenically frozen until such a time as we knew they could get themselves across a street without fucking it up. Most of the men I served with were nineteen. I'm fairly certain that when you were nineteen you couldn't parallel park.

—Do you know that we met once? It was when I was fifteen. Do you remember Boys State?

—Of course. I voted to refund it every year it came up for renewal.

—I went.

—You went to Boys State?

—In Sacramento. 1994. I did all the Boys State things—watched the legislature, learned about democracy, saw some politicians speak. I even ran for lieutenant governor in that mock election.

—How'd you do?

—I lost. I was asked to quit.

—Why?

—Doesn't matter. They were probably right.

—What'd you do?

—There was an essay component to the whole thing, and I thought it would be good to sign mine in blood. Like Thomas Paine.

—I don't think Thomas Paine . . . Anyway. They didn't like that?

—I guess not. They were nice enough about it after I explained myself. But they made me withdraw.

—I can see you're a fan of grand gestures, though.

—Sometimes. I guess so. But that's how we met.

—In Sacramento?

—No, but through Boys State. There was a parade through Marview on the Fourth of July, and you rode in the back of a convertible. I don't know what you were doing out here, but you were in the same car as me. It was some old vintage car, and that year's local Boys State reps were in the car with you. You were exotic that year because you'd come all the way from Wyoming. You remember?

—Sure, I guess. I mean, I've done a couple hundred parades over the years, so I don't know if . . .

—But no one ever comes to Marview. We're just forgotten. People see this broken-down military base and assume anything near it is toxic and dead. I don't know. Maybe it is. Sometimes it is.

—I remember the day being bright.

—I love you for that, sir. Sometimes it was bright here. It really was. This was always some kind of model for diversity and a strong middle class and all that, then the base closed and it all fell down a few notches after that. It's like steroids, right? You ever know a guy on roids?

—I believe so.

—They get huge and the muscles get shiny, right? But when they stop, it all sinks like mud. Round shoulders, potbellies. Saggy breasts.

—Okay.

—But you were right. That day of the parade was bright. And I was sitting next to you, with another kid. We rode for a few hours together through Marview. I even helped you get in and out of the car. You dropped an ice cream cone someone got you and I helped you clean up, wiping your shirt and pants and . . .

—Okay. I remember you.

—So you remember what you said to me that day?

—No, son. I doubt that I do.

—You said that I should play by the rules.

—Okay. I said that to a lot of people.

—And I did it. So where am I?

—And this is some failure of the formula? That you didn't arrive at where you expected to be? And that your astronaut isn't on the Shuttle? That somehow this puts in question the entire framework?

—Yes sir, that's my thesis.

—Well, I have to say, that is a cockamamie thesis. That's like saying that if you lose a certain football game that the sport itself is flawed. Son, not everyone can win the game. Some people play it poorly. Some people quit. Some people don't even read the playbook.

And some people expect the rest of the team to carry them into the end zone.

—No. What I'm saying is that you moved the end zone. And you turned the grassy field into mud.

—I don't know what to say to all that.

—You changed the rules.

—We did not change the rules.

—It just seems chaotic.

—You think it's more chaotic now than *when*? The fucking frontier days? *Then* it was perfectly organized, kid? When people were sleeping on hay and eating squirrels?

—No. But during postindustrial . . .

—Post goddamned *what*? When you had to save a month for a radio? When having indoor plumbing was a sign you'd arrived? Jesus Christ, son, the worst thing your predecessors ever did for you young pricks was to succeed. We made everything so easy that you cry yourselves up a storm every time there's a pebble in your path.

—Okay, at least tell me this: Is it all the same money?

—Is what all the same money?

—The money that could have saved the Shuttle, and the money we send to random countries, that we use to remake unchangeable countries ten thousand miles away.

—Is it the same money?

—Yeah, is it? I mean, you guys complain about not having money for schools, for health care, that everything's broke and we have government shutdowns and every other goddamn thing, and then we look up and you're spending 150 million on air-conditioning in Iraq.

—Listen, you're preaching to the converted here.

—I don't want to be preaching. I'm *asking.* I don't know how that works. Where does the money come from? You guys fight over pennies for *Sesame Street,* and then someone's backing up a truck to dump a trillion dollars in the desert.

—So you're asking where does the money that finances wars come from?

—Yes.

—You're smart enough to know that. We create that money. It's not a standard part of a year's budget. There isn't a line item for war.

—So is it true that we're essentially borrowing money from the Chinese to finance these wars?

—Oh shit. No. But we create and sell bonds, and people here and elsewhere, for example in China, see these bonds as a good investment. And no doubt the Chinese like the leverage it gives them, holding so much American debt.

—But couldn't we just sell bonds to pay for Social Security, education for all, college for all? I mean, everyone wrings their hands about cutting or saving some microscopic government program, and *Where oh where will we get the money?*—but then we turn around and there's a billion dollars for Afghani warlords. I mean, I know I'm stupid not to understand this, but I don't.

—The problem with all those things you mention, education and whatnot, is those are chronic problems, as opposed to acute problems. We fund the things that are urgent, that everyone can rally around and more or less agree upon. And everyone agrees on funding the troops that are stationed abroad. You fund some advisors, then you inch it toward full engagement, and pretty soon no one wants to be the one denying body armor to our young people in uniform. So we find the money. We sell bonds, we borrow money. But will we get that kind of momentum to borrow money from China to pay for some national education reform? No. That's not an acute problem. If there were an alien invasion tomorrow, and the only way to win against the aliens would be to fully fund Head Start, then sure, we would find that money.

—So it's not a matter of possibility, but of will?

—What's that?

—Will.

—Of course. Everything is a matter of will.

—My mom always said that.

—Well, she was right.

—Not often.

—Son, did you bring me here to talk about your mother?

—But don't you think there should be a plan for people like me, for the guys you were talking about, the vets whose brains are scrambled?

—What sort of plan?

—Don't you think . . .

—What, son?

—Don't you think that the vast majority of the chaos in the world is caused by a relatively small group of disappointed men?

—

—

—I don't know. Could be.

—The men who haven't gotten the work they expected to get. The men who don't get the promotion they expected. The men who are dropped in a jungle or a desert and expected video games and got mundanity and depravity and friends dying like animals. These men can't be left to mix with the rest of society. Something bad always happens.

—Something bad like this. Like you bringing me here. I agree.

—When I see these massacres at malls or offices, I think, There by the Lake of God go I.

—Grace of God.

—What's that?

—It's "There but for the grace of God."

—No. It's "there by the Lake of God."

—It's "grace of God."

—It can't be.

—Son. It is.

—I've always had this picture in my mind of the Lake of God. And you walk by it.

—There's no Lake of God.

—It was like this huge underground lake, and it was dark and cool and peaceful and you could go there and float there and be forgiven.

—I don't know what to tell you, son. I've been teaching the Bible for thirty-eight years and there is no Lake of God in that book. There's a Lake of Fire, but I don't think that's the place you're picturing.

—See, even that.

—Even what?

—Even that's a sign that the world has misused people like me. How could I not know that, the difference between the Lake of God and the Lake of Fire?

—I don't know if that misunderstanding is symptomatic of a societal failure. You got your lakes confused.

—But it is symptomatic. You and I read the same books and hear the same sermons and we come away with different messages. That has to be evidence of some serious problem, right? I mean, I shouldn't have been left to live among the rest of society. There were so many days I looked at it all and wanted it wiped away, wanted it on fire.

—Sounds like you had a radicalizing moment, son. Were you beaten as a child, something like that?

—No sir.

—Saw some terrible thing that changed you?

—Do you remember the other guy with us in that car that day?

—No, I can't say that I do.

—You don't? It was unusual for our town to have a kid like that. He was half Vietnamese. Don Banh. You remember a kid like that?

—I'm sorry, I don't. He was a friend of yours?

—He's dead now.

—I'm sorry to hear that.

—He was shot.

—He was a soldier?

—No. Just in his backyard.

—I'm sorry, son. That's too young. I'm truly sorry.

—I'm not saying that was some radicalizing moment for me. I feel like I had some fairly apocalyptic thoughts before that.

—Most young men do.

—I've tried to explain these thoughts to people but they get scared. They don't understand. Or they pretend they don't understand.

—Try me.

—Well, every day, about half of every day I'm among people in a city, I picture my arm sweeping across the city, wiping it all clean. Like it was a model set up on a card table, and I could just sweep it all onto the floor. Okay?

—Okay.

—You want to hear more?

—Sure.

—I'll be walking down some crowded street and I'll start boiling inside and I picture myself parting all these people like Moses with the Red Sea. You know, the people disappear, the buildings dissolve and when I'm done there's all this empty space, and it's quieter, and there aren't all those people and all their dirty thoughts and idiotic talking and opinions. And that vision actually gives me peace. When I picture the landscape bare, free of all human noise and filth, I can relax.

—Maybe you should live in the country.

—That's not funny. I mean, that's not the solution. I just wish I could function better in rooms, in buildings, in a line at the grocery store. And sometimes I do. But sometimes it makes me so fucking tense. I need to get out, drive awhile, get to the ocean as fast as I can.

—Son, I'm realizing I don't know your name.

—Thomas.

—Thomas, nothing you say is unprecedented. There are others like you. Millions of men like you. Some women, too. And I think this is a result of you being prepared for a life that does not exist. You were built for a different world. Like a predator without prey.

—So why not find a place for us?

—What's that?

—Find a place for us.

—Who should?

—You, the government. You of all people should have known that we needed a plan. You should have sent us all somewhere and given us a task.

—But not to war.

—No, I guess not.

—So what then?

—Maybe build a canal.

—You want to build a canal?

—I don't know.

—No, I don't get the impression you do.

—You've got to put this energy to use, though. It's pent up in me and it's pent up in millions like me. The only time I feel right is when I'm driving, or once in a while during a fight.

—So you box?

—No.

—Oh. Let me see your hands.

—They're messed up right now.

—That they are. Son, who are you fighting?

—I don't know. People.

—Do you win?

—Win what?

—These fights.

—No. Not really.

—Thomas, you know we can't round up every confused young man and send them to some remote region. Even if I agreed with you, which I do, to some extent at least. I mean, this is why so many soldiers stay in the Army and why so many prisoners end up back in prison. They cannot hack polite society. They're bored and they feel caged.

—But there's no evidence of a plan, sir.

—What plan?

—Any plan. I mean, wasn't that what Australia was all about? Some convict colony? We could have done that on the moon. All I ever wanted to do was get off this fucking planet and go to the next one, but there's no way to do it. And Don, too. He didn't belong in regular society after what happened to him.

—I don't understand. After he died?

—No, before that. All along I knew what was going to happen. I knew something would happen but I didn't know what. I mean, that's when I first got the idea for all this. We used to mess around here at this base. We'd ride through these buildings on our bikes, and when we were older we'd sit around drinking here, and when Don was losing his shit a little, and he did a few rehabs, I used to think, You know, if I could just shackle him inside one of these buildings for a while, you know, keep him safe, dry him out, then maybe he could make it.

—Okay. I understand that. I truly do.

—But he was always just out there. In the world. Doing the wrong things, never doing anything I told him to do. I always knew what he needed to do, and I'd make a step-by-step for him, I'd even write that shit down. I'd write down a plan! A two-year plan, a five-year plan. And he wouldn't even attempt it. I couldn't make him do anything. I couldn't keep him in rehab. I couldn't lock him up. You know once I left him in jail for a month instead of bailing him out, because I thought it might be good for him? Jail was the safest place.

—Sometimes it truly is.

—I know he'd still be alive if I'd thought of this earlier, if I'd have brought him here and just locked him in one of these buildings until he had his shit straight.

—I understand that, too. This is familiar ground for me.

—I'm just pissed at myself I didn't think of it sooner.

—Of chaining your buddy to a pole.

—Right.

—But you know that's not a durable solution.

—Then what is?

—I don't know. Rehab? Therapy?

—C'mon. Get serious.

—

—Really, why don't we have some kind of plan for people like this? I guess the main government plan is to lock them all up, and I understand the impulse to keep them apart from decent society. I get that. But then there are guys like me and Don, who haven't really done anything wrong, and there are soldiers like the ones you fought with, who come back with these terrible ideas and murdering skills, and there's no place for any of us. We've been out in the wilderness and tasted raw meat, and now we can't sit at the table using utensils. There's got to be someplace for us. A place like this would actually work. This place is 28,000 acres, bordering the ocean. The ground's fertile enough. I mean, you set this land aside for people like us, and I bet you'd reduce crime in this country by half.

—Where are we, did you say?

—I can't tell you that.

—Thomas, what difference does it make?

—Okay. We're at Fort Ord.

—Fort Ord? Like near Monterey?

—You should have deduced that, anyway, sir. There's only one base this big on the coast of California.

—Shit. This is where I did my basic training. You know this is a public place? There'll be hikers through here at first light.

—See, that's so sad.

—What is?

—That you don't know this park is closed. The whole place is locked for the foreseeable future. Budget cuts. The gate at the highway's closed. I just snapped the lock with bolt cutters and put a new one on.

—And the budget cuts are my fault, too.

—No one had a plan for anything. I guess that's the crushing thing, the thing that drives us all crazy. We all think there must be someone very smart at the controls, spending the money, making plans for our schools, parks, everything. But then it's guys like you, who are just guys like me. No one has a fucking clue.

—So we're out here alone?

—I haven't seen a soul here in days.

—It's a beautiful spot.

—You probably didn't see the ice plants out there, but they're everywhere, a dozen colors. They look like some stupid rainbow puked everywhere. And the light is so white here, so weightless and white. Part of me wants to stay here.

—But the longer you keep us here, son, the more likely you'll die here.

—You mean they'll kill me here.

—Son, you must know that's a distinct possibility.

—I know.

—An ever-growing possibility.

—Yeah, I know.

—The longer you keep us here, the more it becomes a near certainty. They will find you, for sure. That is for damned sure. Then they'll do a raid. And because no one will be watching out here, in the middle of nowhere, hell, some sniper might just shoot your head off for fun.

—I know, I know.

—Matter of fact, I *know* that is how it'll go down. I really don't think you'll be taken in alive.

—Yeah, I guess. But things are really clarifying for me out here. I feel like this is really helping me. I'm sorry for the circumstances but I have to say that this has been really helpful so far.

—I don't know what to say to that.

—At first it was just supposed to be Kev, but now having the two of you out here is really making a difference.

—Who's Kev again?

—The astronaut. I thought I just needed to talk to him. But then it came to a point where I had questions for you, and your answers have been really illuminating.

—Okay.

—And I don't mean to be rude, but now I have to go for a while.

As we've been talking I've been thinking of someone else who should be here. I think I should get him while there's time.

—Son, please don't bring anyone else to this place.

—Just this one guy. I think you'd understand if you knew who he was.

—No, I wouldn't. There's no cause for bringing anyone else here. Please, just let us go, turn yourself in, and I can tell the police you were a decent enough young man. I promise to advocate for the best outcome here. I think you need help.

—I know I do. It's just a matter of what kind of help. I'll be back in a bit. Here's your pills. You need water for the pills?

—Yes.

—Okay, I'll just put it here. And here's some granola bars. You're probably hungry. I'll be back in a little bit.

—Son.

—I got to go. But again, I just want to say how sorry I am that you're here under these circumstances. My respect for you could not be greater and I'm really thankful for your kindness so far.

—Son.

—See you soon.

BUILDING 54

—Do you know why you're here?

—No. Where am I?

—I'm not telling you that.

—How did you get me here?

—It wasn't hard. I waited for you to bring out the recycling.

—Oh my god.

—You're locked to that post, and you'll stay there until we're done.

—Don't hurt me.

—I have no plans to do that. This is a deposition.

—A deposition.

—I think you know what it's about.

—I don't. Who are you?

—Maybe you could guess.

—You want me to guess?

—I want you to guess why you're here. There's no way the astronaut or the congressman knew why they were brought here, but you really might have an idea. I actually think you already know.

—I don't.

—You do, though.

—Sir, I don't know what you want.

—Sir? Wow, I like that. I like you calling me *Sir*. Thank you. That actually helps me see you in a more favorable light. Now do you remember me?

—No, I don't. My head hurts so much. And I can't see that far.

—Are these yours? I found them in my bag and I didn't know whose they were. You didn't wear glasses when I knew you.

—You were a student?

—Yes. I was a student in your class. Sixth grade. Ah, I just saw something in your eyes. Some flash of fear. Now do you know why I'm here and you're here?

—No. I don't.

—Okay, now you're defiant again. I heard that about you. I heard you were good. You passed lie detector tests and everything. And the thing is, you really might be innocent. No one knows for sure. That's why you're here.

—

—Now you're not talking. Does it feel weird to be chained to a post?

—

—You really should answer. I haven't had to use the taser yet, but

54

I would use it on you. You're the first one I would not mind using
it on.

—Sir, what are your plans for me?

—Again, I love the *Sir*. I really do. But I have to say, that penitent
tone makes you seem more guilty. You should consider that.

—Please, will you tell me what your plans are for me?

—My plans are to ask you questions and for you to answer them.

—Okay. And then what?

—And then I let you go.

—You'll let me go?

—You and the astronaut and everyone else will be let go. I have
a real astronaut three buildings over. He's an honorable man. And I
have a former congressman. He gave me the idea to find you, indi-
rectly at least. He's an honorable man, too. You, though, I don't know.
Well, I do know. You're not an honorable man. I know that much.
At the very best, you're just sad and twisted. Maybe just lonely. But
I think you're more than that. I think you're a monster. Now do you
know why you're here?

—I think you should just explain it. I don't want to guess.

—You don't want to guess. Okay. Now you just painted yourself
into a corner. That means you did other terrible things. You did so
many terrible things that you don't know which of them this is about.
That's what you just revealed to me. You said that you don't remember *what* you did to me. That it could be any number of crimes.

—I didn't say that.

—You didn't need to.

—Please. Let's stay specific here. I don't remember you, but I trust now that you were a student at Miwok Middle School. Were you one of the students who filed a complaint against me?

—Ah, now suddenly you're all business. Good. You acknowledge that complaints were lodged against you.

—There were seven complaints. Nothing was proven.

—But you left teaching.

—Yes. It was impossible to stay under those circumstances.

—Circumstances you created.

—There was no trial and there was no hearing.

—God, it's like you have it *rehearsed*. I guess you have to. If you talk to a cousin or nephew and they ask you why you left teaching, you have to recite this stuff about "allegedly" and "no hearing" and all that. What did you tell your parents?

—My father is dead. But my mother knows the truth.

—"My mother knows the truth"! Wow. That is a revealing comment. What is the truth, Mr. Hansen?

—The truth about what?

—Yes! You are brilliant! You know how to turn it back to me, to make sure you don't say anything too broad. You don't want to say, for example, that you didn't mean to touch that one kid in the bathroom, because maybe I don't *know* about that one kid in the bathroom. This is fun, Mr. Hansen! You're more fun than the others. I have to draw this out. I have to make sure I don't rush it. Okay, let's see. Do you remember the late eighties, Mr. Hansen?

—Yes, I remember the late eighties.

—Watch the attitude, Mr. Hansen. You're tied to a post. You're ten miles from the nearest highway. I could bludgeon you and you'd never be found. You know this?

—Yes.

—And you're really the first one in this whole process I would actually hurt. I'm guessing you can tell I don't have much to lose, right?

—Yes. I can sense that.

—"I can sense that." That is great. Yes. I'm risking a lot here. Having you and the astronaut and everyone out here. But Jesus, so far, it's been so worth it. I've learned so much. It's like all the pieces are coming together. The one thing I'm kicking myself about is that I didn't do this sooner. You should have been brought here sooner. Twenty years ago. You don't belong with people just like I don't belong with people.

—I trust you have someone you're seeing? A professional?

—Don't talk to me that way. You know I'm making sense. I've done an unusual thing here, but I'm not irrational. You know that. Your undergraduate degree was in psychology. But I guess that never means anything.

—No. Not in my case.

—Isn't that funny, the undergrads who major in psychology? It's like half of every college, these psych majors. They have no idea why they're studying psychology. It's like majoring in faces, or people. "I'm majoring in multiple-choice questions about people."

—Right.

—See, still with the attitude. You have a smarmy way about you, you know that?

—

—Were you always that way? I can't remember.

—I don't know.

—You should be making yourself more appealing, not less, don't you think?

—I suppose so.

—But even your phrasing is smarmy. "I suppose so." Who talks like that?

—I can't help the way I talk.

—Of course you can. Now stop being so smarmy.

—I will try.

—Now that: "I will try." You really should just say "I'll try." Use contractions. Contractions will make you sound more like a regular human being.

—Okay.

—Are you one of those assholes who says *either* with the long *i*?

—No.

—That wasn't convincing. I bet you are. You know who says *either* with the long *i*? Assholes.

—Sir, I want to do whatever I can to help you. Why did you bring me here?

—But how can I be surprised that you're an asshole? I brought you here *because* you're an asshole.

—So you were one of the complainants?

—No.

—But you were in my class?

—Yes. Remember me?

—I might if you give me your name.

—No, asshole. But I remember you being the fun teacher. Was that your goal, to seem like the cool one, the fun one?

—I don't know.

—You dressed like us. Or tried to dress young at least. I remember you wearing Jordache jeans. Do you remember wearing Jordache jeans?

—I don't know.

—You wear Jordache jeans and don't remember? That's not something you forget. That's a full commitment. They were made for women, so when a man wore them, it was all-out. There was no half-way to those pants. That's a major life decision you wouldn't forget. Now tell me if you wore Jordache jeans.

—I believe I did.

—See, where does a worm like you come from? First you wear Jordache jeans. Then you deny it. Then, when you admit it, you say, "I believe I did."

—Sir, what does this have to do with anything?

—It has everything to do with everything. You were trying to insinuate yourself. You were trying to garner our trust. You were trying to seem like us, our age, harmless, cool.

—I don't know about that.

—Then you could get the babysitting jobs.

——

—Right?

——

—Do you remember babysitting for Don Banh?

—Yes.

—Good. That was good. A straight answer. You did overnights.

—Yes.

—When their parents were gone for a week or whatever, you would stay with the kids, feed everyone, tuck everyone in at night, sleep over. You remember?

—Yes.

—What were the Banh kids' names?

—Don, John, Christina, Angelica.

—So you remember them.

—Of course I do.

—Funny how selective your memory is.

—

—Do you remember me coming over while you babysat?

—No.

—You liked to wrestle. I remember coming over one night and walking into the basement and you were there wrestling with Don and John. You were all sweating.

—

—So why the wrestling, Mr. Hansen?

—Were we clothed?

—What?

—Were we clothed?

—Yes. You were. So what?

—I just want to stick to what happened and what you saw. If we're going to do this, I want to stick with facts, and not conjecture and insinuation.

—I can't believe this. You're on the offensive.

—I'm trying to keep us factual.

—Good. Good, motherfucker. I want to be factual, too. Good.

—So let me ask you a question.

—You're going to ask *me* a question?

—May I?

—May you? Mother may you? Fuck yeah, go ahead.

—Did your father ever wrestle with you?

—You weren't their father.

—But did your father wrestle with you?

—Yes. Probably. I didn't see him much after I was six.

—And where was the Banhs' father?

—I don't know.

—He was gone. I was the primary male presence in their lives.

—So you thought, These poor fatherless boys need a grown-up man to take them into the basement for some sweaty wrestling.

—I did everything a parent would do. When they were in my care, I fed them, got them ready for school, made sure they brushed their teeth. And we played any number of games, including just horsing around.

—You know what? You shouldn't say that. Horsing around implies things you don't want to imply. You sound guilty with words like that.

—Thomas, what is it that you think I did?

—Wait. Now you know my name?

—I've been scanning my mind, and I found you.

—Oh shit. You are terrifying. The way you said that. "I found you." Do you know how you sound? I don't want you using my name.

—That's fine. But again, what do you think I did?

—The same thing all the complainants said you did.

—Did you ever read the complaints, Thomas?

—I told you not to use my name.

—I'm sorry. Did you read the complaints?

61

—I read *about* them.

—What do you think they said?

—That you diddled kids. That you're a molester.

—Do you really think the complaints said that?

—Yes.

—And if the complaints said that, they would just let me walk away? No charges? No prison?

—It was a different time.

—It might have been a different time, but if I'd been accused of molestation, they would not have allowed me to just retire and live in the next town over.

—So why did you quit teaching?

—I had to quit. The insinuations were distracting to everyone.

—So you quit on your own volition? To save everyone from distraction?

—That's correct.

—No one asked you to quit?

—No one did. We all discussed it, though, and I was the first to bring up the possibility of me resigning.

—You brought it up.

—I believe so.

—You "believe so." Hansen, your mouth keeps making mistakes. Okay though. I want to get back to all that. But let's walk through this first. Do you remember me coming to your house?

—No.

—God. I feel like hitting you so badly.

—I *don't* remember. *Did* you come to my house?

—I did.

—Okay.

—It's not okay, Mr. Hansen. What the fuck is a "math party"?

—

—See. Now you're scared. You fucking sick fuck.

—Stop. Don't get ahead of yourself.

—Don't get ahead of myself?

—I'm sorry for my tone. But you said we would stick to facts, and what happened, and what you personally saw.

—Right. It was 1989. I was eleven. I was with Don Banh and Peter Francis. Do you remember inviting us over to your house for a "math party"?

—Yes.

—Yes?

—Yes.

—Well shit. That is fascinating. You said yes! That is amazing. Well, that's the first time you've demonstrated some spine. So you do remember it.

—I remember it. But I don't specifically remember you being at my house.

—Okay, fine. But what the fuck is a math party, Mr. Hansen?

—I fed you kids, and we did math homework.

—Really? That was it?

—That was the primary purpose.

—Well now you're a liar again. That was the primary purpose? That was the primary purpose? Don't fuck with me. You're saying that your great idea was to invite sixth-grade boys over to your house and teach us math? That this couldn't be done after school or in a classroom or anything vaguely appropriate? That it had to be at your house, at night, and we had to sleep over? That this was a great idea? The primary purpose was math?

—Yes. I taught math, and this was a way for some students to catch up on concepts they didn't understand.

—Why did we sleep over, Mr. Hansen?

—I don't know. Probably because you all were having fun.

—How many beds were in that house, Mr. Hansen?

—In the house I lived in then?

—Yes.

—I don't know.

—I'm about to kick you in the head.

—Three.

—Good. Do you remember where we all slept that night?

—No.

—Don't make me get up.

—I'm assuming you're upset because you slept in my bed.

—Why the fuck did we sleep in your bed, Mr. Hansen?

—I don't know. I'm guessing we fell asleep watching a movie. That's the real reason why you kids wanted to come over, because I'd let you watch scary movies.

—I didn't like scary movies.

—Well, then I don't know why you came over. Why *did* you come over?

—I came over because my crazy mother heard Don was going, and she thought you'd help me with my math. She thought it was some honor to come to your fucking math party. Did you rape us, you sick fuck?

—No.

—Mr. Hansen, I haven't harmed anyone out here. But you're making a strong case for getting your head kicked in.

—I didn't hurt you. I didn't even undress you, any of you.

—You didn't undress us.

—No. I promise you. I did not.

—Okay. I want to table that for a second. We'll come back to the clothes. First I want to get back to the beds. Don told me he came to four of your math parties. And each time he remembers being carried to your bed and then to another bed where he woke up. Why did you move him around?

—He probably remembers wrong. The kids typically fell asleep in my bed.

—Watching movies.

—Right. And then I'd carry them to the guest room.

—Well that sounds positively innocent.

—I know it doesn't sound innocent.

—How *do* you think it sounds?

—I think it sounds inappropriate.

—Did you know it sounded inappropriate *then*?

—Yes.

—So why did you do it?

—Why did I invite you over for movies?

—Yes.

—I was lonely.

—That's it?

—Thomas, are you planning to harm me?

—No. I don't know. Maybe. I'm vacillating between wanting to harm you and feeling bad for you. Why?

—Thomas, if you give me your word that you won't harm me, I can fill in the details of the night you spent at my house. I understand why you'd want to know what exactly happened. I can do that. But I won't do it if you're going to kill me irregardless.

—That's not a word. You should know that. You're a teacher.

—What's not a word?

—Irregardless. It's just like saying *either* with the long *i*. You think you sound smarter, but you sound stupider. You should just stick to regular words. Don't stretch.

—Okay. Sorry.

—Don't be sorry. Just be smarter. You want to know whether I'll guarantee your safety. Well, let's see. I have to say . . . no. I can't guarantee anything. I don't owe you that.

—Thomas, I didn't harm you. I didn't harm Don.

—I don't believe you. And don't say my name.

—Okay. Then why did you bring me here?

—What do you mean?

—You went to a lot of trouble to get me here. But you're rejecting my offer to fill in the gaps in your memory. I want you to have peace with this. You're not the first former student to come to me wanting to know about those nights.

—And what did you tell them?

—The same thing I'm telling you. That what I did was inappropriate but that nothing terrible happened. You were not raped.

—See, this is what I don't understand. Why risk your job and going to jail and everything else to bring boys to your house if you weren't going to rape us?

—I told you. I was lonely. And it wasn't just boys.

—You brought girls, too?

—Thomas, I need your assurance you won't harm me, and that you'll let me go. I have people in my life who count on me and who need me. My mother lives with me. She's ninety-one. I feed her. I'm guessing it's the afternoon now, so she'll already be wondering where I am.

—You know, Mr. Hansen, you just made a tactical mistake. You fucked up, you fucked with the minds of however many kids who were under your care, and now you're making demands of me.

—I didn't mean it to come off like a demand. I was just trying to give you a sense of the other people in my life. You had an experience with me twenty years ago, but much has happened since.

—Okay, I understand you were trying to humanize yourself there. I know. If I know about your ancient mother, it supposedly makes it harder for me to harm or kill you. But in this case that's stupid. I already know you're a human being. And I know that you're a monster. And now I know you have a ninety-one-year-old mother, who we both know has lived a long life, and besides, she raised a twisted man. So I'm not overflowing with sympathy.

—You won't guarantee my safety.

—No. But I will say that if you tell me everything, and if what you tell me seems credible, then I'll be more likely to leave you alone than if you keep telling me about your ninety-one-year-old mother who raised a pederast.

—I'm not a pederast.

—You invited boys to sleep over and you're not a pederast?

—I acted inappropriately, I know this. But there are degrees to everything.

—You're so sick.

—Thomas. You're a smart guy. And given you've chained me to a post, I know you understand moral choices that are a bit off the beaten path. So I hope you'll understand what I mean when I say that there is a good deal of grey in the world. It's not a popular belief, I know, but most of the world is grey. I know that if a man touches a boy's ass once, he can be labeled a pedophile forever, but that's not fair, either. We've lost all nuance.

—We've lost all nuance? We've lost all nuance? You want to talk about nuance now? What the fuck does this have to do with nuance?

—You've brought me here because you assume that because I invited boys to sleep over, that I raped them. But I did not do that.

—So why bring them to your house? That's the part I don't get.

—Thomas, tell me something. You're a single man?

—Yes.

—Are you straight?

—Yes.

—Have you brought women back to your apartment?

—Yes.

—Did you have sex with each one?

—What? No.

—Then why bring them home?

—That's a stupid analogy.

—Did anyone ever mistake your intentions?

—What do you mean?

—When you got them home, was there ever confusion about your intentions? Did anyone ever think you planned to force your will onto them?

—No.

—I assumed not.

—Fuck you.

—But you could have. That could have been your intention.

—No. It couldn't have been.

—But maybe something goes wrong. Maybe you brought twenty women to your apartment, and let's say each encounter was safe and consensual.

—Yes. They all were.

—But what if the twenty-first encounter wasn't? What if, during that one encounter, you both were drunk and there was confusion about consensuality? And later she accused you of date rape. If you're arrested, or tried, or even just accused, immediately there's doubt about the other encounters, the other twenty, right? Who knows what your intentions were. Maybe you raped them all. Or maybe you tried to. To the outside world, and to all the women who had consensual relations with you, your intentions are suddenly unclear, even in hindsight. Suddenly, to everyone, you're capable of terrible things.

—Not possible.

—But of course it is. An accusation alone puts your entire character in doubt. This is how it works. An accusation is ninety percent of it. Anyone can ruin anyone with an accusation. And people are only too happy to be able to write someone off, to throw them into the pile of the depraved and subhuman. One less person. There are too many people, the world is too crowded. We're suffocating, right? And clearing some of them away lets us breathe. Each person we throw away fills our lungs with new air.

—You're getting off topic.

—I don't think so. You have to realize that you're a victim of this thinking, too. You heard something about me, and you brought me here, fully expecting me to conform to your idea of a throwaway person. But I'm not a throwaway person, am I?

—I don't know yet.

—But we put no value on each other, do we? There are too many people. There are too many people in any given city, any given country. Certainly there are too many people on this planet, so we're so anxious to throw away as many of them as possible. Given any excuse at all, we can erase them.

—

—What if there were only ten of us on Earth? What if there were only ten people you had to choose from who had to help rebuild civilization after some apocalypse?

—Oh Jesus. What's your point?

—My point is that if there were only ten people on Earth, there's no way that you would think I was dispensable. If I had wrestled with Don and had kids over to my house, you would never think those crimes so unforgivable that you'd send me away. I would still be useful. You'd talk to me, you'd work it out. But with so many people, no one person is worth so much. We can clear away wide swaths of people like they were weeds. And usually we do it based on suspicion, innuendo, paranoia. Whole classes of people. Including anyone vaguely associated with pedophilia. They don't get fair trials, they're sent away, and when they try to come back, they can't even live. They live under bridges, in tents, huddled together.

—I don't know what this has to do with you and boys.

—I'm not a rapist. You're presupposing that anyone I brought into my house I intended to rape. But that wasn't the case. Just as it wasn't the case that you intended to have sex with every woman who ever entered your home. Your argument is circumstantial.

—But why bring the kids to your house? Why not just meet them after school?

—Why don't you meet every woman in, say, a public park?

—Because I might want some privacy.

—Am I, too, allowed privacy?

—Not with kids.

—Is any adult allowed to be alone with any child?

—Yes. Listen. You made whatever point you meant to make. And I don't care. Now you have to tell me about the tailor game.

—The what game?

—See? Your face just tensed up. You didn't think I'd remember. Do you remember the measuring tape?

—Yes. The tailor game was also inappropriate.

—Tell me what happened.

—I had a measuring tape and we measured each other's arms and legs and shoulders.

—You don't think that's sick?

—It's inappropriate.

—I can't have anyone crouch near me without thinking of you holding that measuring tape against my leg. When people kneel down to tie their shoes anywhere close to me I think of you.

—That couldn't be my fault.

—Of course it's your fault! You think I had a problem with all that before you and your fucking tailor game?

—Okay, I'm sorry.

—That's it? You're sorry?

—I'm sorry, but tell me this: Did I touch you?

—I have no idea. I assume you did.

—But there you go again. Your mind is filling in what didn't happen. You're filling in with what you *assume* were my intentions. But I never touched any of you kids.

—But you wanted us to touch *you.*

—That's not true either.

—You had us measure your inseam, too, you fucker. Why would you have us measure your inseam if you didn't want us to touch your dick?

—Do you remember touching me there?

—No, but I assume we all did. I remember looking up at you and you were looking at the ceiling, like you could barely contain yourself. You were about to jizz.

—Thomas, I admit it was a little thrill when you would measure my inseam, but I didn't actually have any of you touch me. I did not touch you and you didn't touch me. It was all highly inappropriate, yes, no doubt about it. But I was acutely aware of the law, and I did not break any laws. It wasn't rape. It wasn't assault. I acted inappropriately, and that's why they asked me to resign, which I did. And that was the correct punishment. I didn't belong in a school, and it was decided I should leave, and I did.

—So you went on to do it elsewhere.

—No, I did not. You have to stop making these leaps. I'm not part of some larger narrative. I'm me. I am one person, and my story is absolutely unique. I don't conform to any established modus operandi. I'm not a priest who was shuffled around from church to church or whatever narrative has been established in your mind. I was asked to resign, and I did, and I was relieved.

—You were *relieved*?

—I was. Being around all of you was too much of a temptation. But once I left, the temptations were removed.

—That is really hard to believe.

—But you must believe it. I'm chained to a post, and I'm telling you the truth.

—But it defies belief. It defies all known pathology. A pederast who just reforms himself? It's not possible.

—Thomas, do you know anything about addiction psychology?

—No.

—Well, this conversation is reminiscent of my time in AA. For a while, probably while dealing with my own proclivities, I was occasionally drinking too much. And my AA friends were convinced I was an alcoholic. They brought me to meetings, and they insisted that I quit drinking for good. But I was not an alcoholic. They couldn't accept that even though I used alcohol to cope sometimes, it didn't mean I was out of control or that alcohol was hampering or altering my path through life.

—I don't know what this has to do with you and your tendencies toward boys.

—The point is that it's similarly polarized. The thinking is similarly flawed, and it makes people crazy. Tell me, do you have any friends who are alcoholics?

—Yes.

—Are they all the same?

—No.

—Do they all go on three-day benders and kill people in drunk-driving car accidents?

—No.

—Do they all lose their jobs and families because they can't quit drinking? Because they're drinking twenty-four hours a day?

—No.

—So are you sure they all have the same disease?

—I don't know.

—If I walked into an AA meeting and suggested that I had a "problem" with alcohol but was not an alcoholic, they would run me out of the building. And yet maybe I do have a small problem. Maybe, twice a year, I have one more drink than I should, and I say something I regret. Maybe once or twice a year I pass out, alone, at home, after drinking too many Manhattans. Once a year I drive home when I should take a cab. Am I an alcoholic? Many would say yes. Many would say you either are or are not. They use that old chestnut, *You can't be a little pregnant.* You know that one?

—Yes.

—It's trotted out in situations where nuance is unwelcome.

—Like yours.

—Right. I'm not an alcoholic, and I'm not a rapist. I'm a flawed person who has wandered into territory that could be very dangerous, but then I wandered back to a less problematic path. You can call me a sick man. I am. You can say I did a number of things I should not have done. But I am not a rapist and not a pederast. And I have never touched any naked part of a child, nor have I asked them to touch any naked part of me.

—But you twisted the minds of many people.

—Did I?

—Of course you did.

—Can I give you a corollary?

—Can you give me a corollary?

—Yes.

—Sure. Give me a corollary, you sick fuck.

—When I was growing up there was a house on my street that was overrun with foliage. You could hardly see the house through all the trees and ivy. But this house was known by us kids as the place where you could go and get candy. You could just knock on the door and this older woman would invite you inside and you could choose candy from a bowl. Now this, today, would seem wildly inappropriate, right?

—Yes.

—And telling that story to anyone, which I've done over the years, has always provoked disgust. People assume that any child walking inside that place was a victim and that the woman had some ulterior motive. That there were cameras somewhere, that there was some sick purpose to her inviting us in. It all fits some narrative that's now so well established that it's crowded out all other possibilities. There was the green-shrouded house, the gingerbread look of it. You assume dark and terrible things are happening inside. But they weren't.

—How do you know?

—Because they never did. I've talked to a dozen others who knew the house and went inside and nothing ever happened to any of them. The lady just wanted it to be Halloween every day. She was lonely. But we could never accept that now. We categorize everything with such speed and finality that there's never any room for nuance. Let me posit that the mind-twisting you speak of comes from outside, not within. That is, those who want to name things, to sweep them into categories and label them, have swept your experience into the same category as those children who were actually raped, those who were lured into showers and thrown against the wall and had a grown man's penis inserted into their rectum repeatedly.

—See, just your ability to talk that way . . .

—Thomas, this is important. Is playing tailor fully dressed the same as having a penis thrust into your twelve-year-old rectum?

—See, you are sick. Only a sick fuck could have said that.

—I'm trying to make clear the difference between what I did and what an actual rapist does. I couldn't even undress you boys. Doesn't that make clear that I'm not the same kind of monster?

—Maybe you're a different kind of monster. But you're still a monster.

—I won't accept that. You came over to my house. Don came over to my house. We watched movies. We played tailor. Then you fell asleep on my bed. You woke up and went home. That is the work of a monster?

—Absolutely. We trusted you and you had other intentions toward us. You used us.

—And what would you call what you're doing to me?

—I'm asking you questions. You harmed me, and this is the least amount of payback imaginable.

—How about the astronaut? You kidnapped him to ask him questions. But he did nothing to you.

—Don't worry about the astronaut. I haven't harmed the astronaut. You're the only one I would even think of harming.

—You would be harming someone who harmed no one.

—That is fucking insane.

—I did nothing but imagine them.

—So you admit that you got sexual excitement from children.

—Of course I did. Don't you ever see a woman on the street and later masturbate thinking about them?

—

—Well, I do the same thing. My fantasies might be sick, but I can't make it work any other way. The machinery of my mind is what it is. And mine is warped; it is societally unacceptable. But I know that touching a child, that acting on these desires, is wrong, and I have done nothing illegal.

—You don't buy child porn.

—I don't anymore.

—You don't *anymore*?

—When I was younger I did. But I realized how it impacted actual children, so I stopped. The last time I saw an image of a naked child was 1983.

—So since then you just see a boy on the street and then imagine him naked?

—Not exactly.

—Then what exactly?

—This level of detail isn't useful, is it?

—This level of detail is exactly why you're here.

—Okay. I think of a boy measuring my inseam.

—Oh god. Like how old is this boy?

—The same age you were. Eleven, twelve. That's why we played the game.

—So you could store up those images for later masturbation.

—Yes.

—And all these years since, you're still thinking of Don Banh measuring your inseam?

—Not so much him. Listen, I know it's sick. I wish my brain worked in a different way. I know it's wrong, that it's considered sick. But none of this extends beyond the confines of my head, Thomas. I swear to you.

—So that's it? For twenty years, you just think of boys measuring your inseam? No action taken?

—That's right. Listen. I am sorry that you came to my house. And that Don came to my house, and anyone else. I can never rectify the fact that I acted inappropriately and that I scarred you kids in some way. But again, there are limits to the blame I can assume for whatever else happened in your lives after that.

—But why Don?

—Don was from a certain kind of home. You must know that those who seek to be close to boys seek out those whose parents are missing or inattentive, or who have certain blind spots.

—So Don's mom thought this was some great honor, that you'd invite him over to your house.

—Yes. She trusted me, and she valued my mentorship.

—Your mentorship. Holy shit.

—Again, you'll find it unacceptably complex, but I spent many hundreds of hours with Don and his brother, and most of that time was in the role of a parent. I cooked for them, I helped them with their homework, I took care of them. I was a male figure in their lives where there was no other.

—A male figure who masturbated thinking of them measuring your inseam.

—Yes.

—You're right. It's unacceptably complex. And so wait—was I one of these kids, too? With the parents who were absent and had blind spots?

—I don't know.

—But you do. Don't worry about offending my mom.

—I don't remember your mom, but I assume that at the time, I had a sense that your home was not as strong as others.

—So I was a target. Did you make a list or something?

—A list?

—Of targets. Kids you had identified as potential sleepover participants.

—Yes.

—Yes? You said yes?

—Because this was so long ago, and because I want to be completely candid with you, and because this was part of a life I abandoned and for which I have only shame, I will continue to be honest with you. I had a list every year of the new sixth graders who I designated as potential guests at my house.

—Based on just the parental situation?

—That, and height, hair, looks.

—What kind of looks?

—Any boys who were too tall or developed weren't part of the list. I liked long hair. There were parameters physically, and then I cross-referenced that with the parental factors.

—And this ended up being a list of how many every year?

—Maybe eight, ten kids.

—And these you would invite over.

—Yes.

—And of them how many would come over?

—Maybe three, four.

—And that was enough?

—Yes. And from the three or four, I might get closer with one.

—One like Don.

—Right.

—And when did you start babysitting for them?

—A few months later. Don's mom was going back to Vietnam to visit her family, and she asked me to stay with the kids.

—Lucky you.

—Yes.

—And I was on your list, too.

—I assume so.

—But somehow I didn't get to the next level.

—Well, presumably your parents . . .

—It was just my mom.

—Either your mom sensed something weird about the sleepovers or you did. You said you came over just once?

—Yes.

—That usually meant that there was a sense from someone that it was not right.

—Were you ever scolded? Any dad who would have found out about this would have murdered you.

—No, not always. Some dads cooperated fully.

—God.

—But yes, it was easier when there were no dads in the picture.

—But so someone would question the sleepovers, and that kid would be removed from the rotation?

—Yes. Maybe in your case your mom . . .

—Not my mom. She was completely out of it.

—Well, then maybe it was you.

—I don't know. I wish I could remember.

—See? The fact that you can't remember proves that the harm to you was minimal.

—You're in no position to make assumptions like that.

—

—So you think there was something wrong with my mom?

—Excuse me?

—You targeted me because of my mom?

—I have no idea. I'm only saying that typically there was something missing at home that allowed me some degree of access.

—Okay. Okay.

—I've told you all I can.

—Your candor was helpful to your situation here.

—So you'll free me now?

—No.

BUILDING 55

—Do you know who I have next door?

—Where am I?

—You're in a military barracks. Do you know who I have next door? You'll never guess.

—Oh God.

—Shh. Guess.

—Thomas, what have you done to me?

—You're locked to the post there, but it's okay. It's just to keep you safe.

—Oh Jesus lord Christ. Thomas, you have lost your mind.

—You know what's so funny? I didn't even need the chloroform with you. You never woke up. What the hell are you on? It couldn't be just Paxil and wine. You must be mixing it with something else.

—Thomas, don't do what I think you're going to do.

—What do you think I'm going to do?

—I won't say.

—You think I'm planning to kill you or something?

—I don't know. I don't know why I'm here. How did you get me here?

—You don't remember?

—I don't know if I do.

—Of course you don't. You were passed out when I got to the house. It was the easiest thing. I put you in the van and then on the cart and that was that.

—Oh God.

—Stop. Don't moan like that.

—Oh God oh God.

—Enough of that. Please.

—I can't believe this.

—Believe it and let's get started.

—Thomas, why would you do this?

—I know it seems extreme. I'm sorry. I really am.

—Jesus Christ.

—But you know I'm a principled person.

—Oh God.

—And this is the best way to get some things resolved.

—Oh Thomas. Please.

—Stop that. Don't blubber.

—I'm chained here like a dog!

—I've chained everyone the same way.

—Thomas, this is how you treat your mother? Seriously, how did you get me here?

—I'm capable of lots of things you wouldn't even know.

—Like kidnapping.

—Mom, I can do extraordinary things. I brought an astronaut here. He's still here. I did that myself. You're the fourth person I've brought. You know Mac Dickinson, the congressman? He's here, too.

—Oh no. No.

—See, you can never give me any credit.

—Thomas, you've really lost it. They'll catch you and put you in prison for life. Is this why you were at the house? I heard you skulking around and figured you were just taking something from the garage. I saw your car.

—Then what? You passed out? That is the best. That sums it up.

—Thomas, why did you do this?

—I had to. There was a vise around my head and now it's easing.

—I blame myself.

—For once you do.

—What does that mean?

—It's just amazing to hear you accept blame for anything.

—Like what?

—Like what? Like what? There you go. You're back to denying the calamity all around. How do you do it?

—Ow. Damn it, Thomas.

—You shouldn't pull on that.

—Thomas, see what this is doing?

—Then don't move. It makes the shackle feel tighter. The whole setup works best if you just sit in one place. Especially at your age.

—Look at my ankle! It's already purple.

—It's not purple.

—Thomas, it would work best if you just unlocked this whole thing and we could really just sit and talk.

—Guess who I have next door.

—No, I won't. I don't want to know. An astronaut. A congressman. You told me.

—Yes, I have those guys. But guess who else?

—I don't know, Thomas. The idea of you kidnapping all these people makes me want to vomit. I can't believe my son would do this.

—You act like you had nothing to do with it.

—You're saying there was something in my raising of you that would make you into a kidnapper? That is absurd.

—Absurd? Mom, *everything* you did brought me to this place.

—See, you were born ready to blame others for your mistakes.

—No, Mom. No.

—Thomas, it's the truth. I've always felt the same way. I knew you were screwy. Always. You were screwy out of the womb. You were screwy as a child, screwy as an adolescent.

—Well, that's a nice coincidence, because I have a remnant of that period in the barracks next door.

—Who?

—Think of sixth grade.

—I have no idea. Not Mr. Hansen.

—I knew you knew.

—You kidnapped Mr. Hansen.

—He was a lot easier than the astronaut. Almost easier than the congressman. He was so pliant. Weak.

—Son, I hope you didn't harm that man. They'll kill you if you did anything to Dickinson.

—Of course I didn't. He's an honorable man. Like me, like Kev. You don't get the point of all this at all.

—That's right, Thomas. I don't.

—So do you remember sending me to Mr. Hansen's house?

—I know you went there. I don't remember *sending* you there. Now Thomas, let me out of this.

—Of course you sent me there.

—All your friends were going. Thomas, please take these handcuffs off.

—All my friends? Hardly. Don Banh went. He's the only normal kid I remember ever going there, and he went because his mom spoke no English and thought it was the way to get Don better grades. You know Mr. Hansen targeted kids whose parents were absent or incompetent in some way?

—I don't know where you get this anger.

—You don't think I have anything to be angry about? Mom, what kind of parent lets their son go to "math overnights"? Doesn't that seem irresponsible?

—It didn't seem irresponsible at the time. You begged me to go. You *begged* me.

—No. No. No. No. No. You came home one day and you'd heard about this "opportunity" to go to Mr. Hansen's house for enrichment. You thought it would help me, would get him to like me. You remember what you said? You said, "You could use a friend on the faculty at your school."

—I didn't say that.

—Then how the hell would I remember it after all these years?

—Your memory has always been given to opportunistic revision.

—You're such a monster. Just the way you can say things like that. You know the statements like that I have in my head? *Opportunistic revision!* Jesus, that's the one talent you have—saying nasty, nasty, unforgettable things.

—If I say I'm sorry will you let me go?

—No.

—Thomas, I'm worried about you. How long have you had the astronaut and the congressman?

—So you believe me.

—Of course I do. That's what's so scary.

—Well that's a start at least. I didn't think you'd believe I was capable of it.

—I know you are. I knew it when you burned the hospital.

—See, why would you say that? I didn't burn any hospital.

—Thomas, please.

—Please? Please what? Who said I burned that hospital? I was never accused of that.

—Thomas.

—What?

—It adds up. You've kidnapped me. You're capable of radical acts. Now it all connects.

—I can't believe you'd make an accusation like that in your position.

—I'm your mother.

—But you're shackled to a post.

—I'm still your mother and I know things. Children are utterly transparent to their mothers. I knew every time you did something. When the playground down the street was graffitied, I knew it was you. Your handwriting was obvious.

—See, you lie. If you'd thought that was me, you would have said something.

—I wasn't in the best of shape those years.

—But you are now?

—You know I'm better.

—I don't know that. You're never better. You know how many times I wanted to do something like this with you, get you and lock you somewhere so you couldn't do anything stupid? So you couldn't mix meds and drive around, running into telephone poles? I dreamed of it since I was twelve. Just to have you locked up till you were clean.

—Well, I'm glad you didn't. You would have been locked up yourself. As you will be when this is all over.

—Don't threaten me.

—I'm not threatening, Thomas. I'm just stating the obvious. This one goes beyond any of the other petty crimes. This one means you'll never be outside again. How many people did you take altogether?

—Including you, four so far. And I have one or two left.

—You'll get twenty years for each crime. I won't visit you in prison. I can't handle it.

—I'm not going to prison.

—Don't you dare kill yourself.

—That's not what I mean. I'll be gone.

—Thomas, you won't survive wherever you plan to go. You don't stand a chance.

—I don't stand a chance? You're telling me this? You can't tell me about survival. I barely survived *you*.

—You did fine. You're tall, you're healthy.

—I'm tall? I'm healthy? That's your defense? You did a good job with me because I'm tall and don't have leprosy? You are phenomenal.

—Thomas. My point is that you turned out all right. Outside of this and the hospital, you've been fine. You're functional.

—I'm functional? That was your goal, to raise a son who was *functional*? A tall and functional son? Your ambition is incredible. Do you remember what you did with our family photos?

—Excuse me?

—The family albums. Do you remember that?

—Of course I do. You bring it up every few years.

—I've brought it up once, and you were probably high when I last did. One of your boyfriends, whose name was actually Jimmy, stole them when he cleaned out our house. Do you remember this?

—Of course I remember.

—I have no idea why he needed to clean out the whole house. He took everything. He took my bed, my stuff, my clothes. He took my backpack. He took my homework.

—Well, first of all, he didn't do it himself. He hired someone, Thomas, and they didn't know what to take or not to take.

—You know this? You know he hired someone?

—Yes. He told me.

—He told you afterward that he hired someone?

—Yes. I called him because I knew it was him, and I asked him why the hell he had to take everything from that house, instead of just the TV and the stereo.

—I can't believe this. You spoke to him afterward?

—I was trying to get our belongings back.

—Why the hell would he have taken that stuff in the first place?

—We owed him money. I've told you that.

—*We* owed him money? I was thirteen.

—You were old enough to contribute if you'd wanted to.

—Holy shit. Holy shit.

—Stop jumping around. You look like an idiot.

—You're the one chained to a post. *You* look like an idiot.

—Please free me, Thomas. I'm sixty-two. You have a sixty-two-year-old woman chained up. Are you proud of that?

—And never insult me again. You get that? Never again. You've called me an idiot a thousand times and that was the last.

—You're about to hit me.

—No. Even touching you would make me sick. You owed money to someone named Jimmy. You sold our belongings to pay him back. You sold my belongings. And now you say it was my fault.

—I didn't say that. I am not saying that at all. His taking our belongings was not your fault. And when I came home and saw he'd done that, I called him immediately and told him it was out of line.

—Out of line. Holy God.

—He hadn't done it himself. He hired some men.

—This is so much sicker than I ever would have thought. How much did you owe him?

—Three months' rent.

—And that was what? A thousand dollars?

—Twelve hundred.

—And you had no one to borrow it from. No way to work for it. Were you employed at the time?

—I was on disability. You know I had my injury.

—Your injury. Your injury, holy shit.

—You want to look at my arm? It's still healed wrong.

—And I should have contributed to the household income.

—I didn't say that. All I'm saying is that some young men do work. In many parts of the world, you would have been considered the man of the house and expected to contribute.

—You are so great. One in a billion. You know, the reason I was bringing up all this was to note that in all my life I've seen no more than ten pictures of my childhood, but you're making it all so much more fascinating. I give you a chance to explain one thing, and you remind me about a hundred other examples of your insanity. Your crimes multiply every time we talk.

—We had plenty of pictures of you.

—Do you know what kinds of pictures we have of me?

—I do know, because I broke my back reassembling those photo albums.

—Stop. Stop there. I knew the rest of the story, but now I can fill in the beginning. What you did was this. First you date a man named Jimmy, who I believe was a former taxi dispatcher from Salinas and was unemployed when you met him. A man on the way up in society. Then you bring Jimmy into our home and he pretends he's my dad and mentor. He takes me for drives where the windows are closed and he smokes and tells me about how hot his sister is. He says he'll set me up with her even though I was thirteen and she was twenty-eight.

Then somehow you and Jimmy have a falling out. Next thing I know I come home and you're making phone calls on the floor of an empty house. The kitchen plates are gone. The clothes in the closets are gone. My schoolbooks are gone. I go into my room and there's nothing left, nothing but an empty aquarium. You tell me that we were robbed, but somehow I don't believe you. Something seems wrong about that. All our photo albums are gone, so you call up your friends and my friends' parents, and your sisters and cousins and ask everyone to send any pictures they have of me or us.

—I spent weeks on that. Why was that a bad thing to do?

—The result was an album with exactly ten pictures in it. And in every picture, I'm on the side, I'm in the background. These are pictures of my cousins or my friends and I'm incidental. I'm blurry and half my head is cut out.

—I thought I was doing something nice.

—That was my birthday present that year!

—You liked it.

—Oh shit.

—Thomas, I was there when you went to bed and when you woke up. I got you to school. I fed you. Beyond that, you're quibbling.

—Quibbling? See, I guess the one thing I never gave you credit for was how entertaining you are. The things you say are just unprecedented. No one talks like you. Do you remember bringing me to your boyfriend's apartment in New Mexico?

—Of course. He got you a bike.

—He gave me the bike his son left when his wife and kid fled him.

—It was a fine bike, and he bought it for you.

—No he didn't. It had this kid's name on it. Robin.

—Well, we can disagree about that.

—And why take me to Albuquerque in the first place? Why not just leave me with someone?

—You had fun on that trip.

—Your boyfriend hit me.

—Well, you two didn't always see eye to eye.

—I was fifteen. Seeing eye to eye?

—How many times do I need to say sorry for that? It was twenty-five years ago.

—It was less than that.

—So what, Thomas? So what?

—So Mr. Hansen targeted me, knowing I had an addict for a mom. That's how he could get away with it. He needed kids who had some kind of inadequate parental situation. Me, Don.

—Did he touch you, Thomas?

—Who?

—Mr. Hansen.

—He says he didn't.

—Well then.

—"Well then"? "Well then"? You push me onto a highway, or off a bridge, and then if I come back alive, you say, *Well then.*

—Thomas, why don't you unlock me and we can talk about straightening all this out? I can help you get out of here. I'm happy to take the blame for all this. I can tell the police it was my idea, that you weren't here at all.

—That would be the most self-sacrificing thing you've ever done.

—Thomas, we have many more years together. We don't have anyone else. We should look forward. You're always looking backward,
blaming and dissecting, and it's hampered your ability to move ahead.
You need to choose to look to the light.

—Listen to yourself! "Look to the light"? You've always had this
bizarre mix—you're so nasty, but then you spout these New Ageisms.
Don't give me advice.

—I want to be supportive. That's all I want now. You know I'm
better than I used to be. We can be partners.

—We won't be partners. I don't like you.

—We're stuck with each other, Thomas.

—I'm not stuck with you. And you're still using.

—It's under control.

—That's not possible.

—Thomas, I've had the same job for four years. Could I be doing
that if I was out of control?

—You're screwing the owner. I hear that you come into work
twice a week.

—That is patently untrue.

—You always had situations like that, didn't you? You'd screw
some guy who could provide you with some kind of financial assis-
tance or some kind of vague job on someone's payroll. You did that at
the hospital supply company.

—That was a legitimate job. I worked my ass off there. I hated
that job but I did it.

—For a while you did. Maybe six months. Then you were on severance for a year.

—Is it my fault they gave me severance?

—A year's severance for a half year's work? Was that company policy?

—I have no idea.

—And still you dated that guy. Dalton. I can't believe you brought a grown man named Dalton into our house.

—He took you to SeaWorld.

—You have an answer for every one of these guys. You act like every one of them was such a gift to my life.

—You were a lonely boy.

—I was a lonely boy? That's the first time I've heard you say that. What does that mean?

—It means there was only so much I could do with you. You came out of the womb a certain way. You were always diffident. I tried to have you play with other kids but there was always some reason they didn't appeal to you. You went off by yourself and then complained that you had no friends.

—You're making this up.

—I'm trying to tell it to you straight. You want to blame me for everything, fine, but you were always a certain way. On your fourth birthday, you hid in the garage. At your eighth-grade graduation, you stayed in the parking lot, in the car, so I went alone. You never joined the big group activities. I would buy you tickets to everything, sign you up for everything, and you would stay home. How is that my fault? I put you in a position to be happy and you chose to be alone.

—I didn't want to be alone.

—You drove people away. You tried to drive me away.

—I wish I'd been better at it.

—Then why didn't you leave?

—Why didn't I leave?

—Thomas, you lived at home till you were twenty-five.

—You lie. I left when I was twenty-two.

—For eight months. Then you came back.

—For a year.

—No, you came back for two years and eight months. You were twenty-five when you moved out for good. If I was so terrible why come back? Why stay with me so long?

—

—And you couldn't keep a job. You know how easy it is for a white man to make money in this country? It's like falling off a log. For so long I blamed myself for what happened to us. But all along I had a feeling there was something strange about you. And I know I'm right. You were born with certain tendencies, and I really don't think I could have done anything to prevent them. I had a feeling something like this would happen.

—Of course you did.

—You had extreme tendencies. People thought you were gentle and lonely and harmless but I knew a different side of you. When you were seven you choked me. You remember that?

—I didn't choke you.

—You did. This was just after your father left. It was at that rich kid's house. His family had a lot of money. You remember this kid?

—How would I remember something like that?

—I don't know where they got their money, something fishy, but they were sweet to you. He used to have you over to play after school, and he had a playroom and a million toys. They knew I was alone and working so they said you could come over anytime. You don't remember this? They lived on the lake.

—Fine.

—There was one time I picked you up. I used to come to their house and get you after work. And always it was a hassle to get you to leave, but no more than any kid leaving any friend, I figured. But this time you were really resisting. You wouldn't come, and I was standing there in the doorway to the kid's room, with his mom, just trying to chat and be casual while trying to get you to put on your jacket and come with me. But you wouldn't move. I think you thought maybe I'd just leave and let you *live* there. I mean, it made no sense because obviously you have to leave at some point. So finally it starts getting embarrassing, and the mom, I can't remember her name, something like Aureola, she says she has to get something in the kitchen or something. She knew I might need some time alone with you. So she left, and she brought her son with her. Then it was just you and me alone in his room. And I got down on my knees and brought you close to me, and I whispered in your ear that we needed to go. I used to do that in public, get you close and whisper sort of urgently in your ear when you were misbehaving. And so I cupped my hand around your ear and whispered a few choice things about us needing to leave, you embarrassing us, how you'd be punished if you didn't comply, and then I backed up a bit to look into your eyes and make sure you understood, and that's when this look came over your face and you tried to strangle me.

—I did not.

—But you did. Why else would I remember it twenty-five years later? You put your hands around my neck and squeezed. I don't even know where you learned how to do that. I'd never been so scared. Just the look in your eyes! It was pure hatred, pure evil. But then you held on. You were so strong and I couldn't get your hands off me and then your eyes went dull, like a snake's when it's got something in its jaws. You know how they have some mouse in their jaws but their eyes stay open and seem so far away? That was the look you had.

—You're making all of this up.

—So finally I got free, and I spanked you, and you still struggled. I had to carry you out kicking and screaming. You scratched my face and it took a month to heal. I mean, this was terrifying. Can you imagine? You never went back to that house. I was too embarrassed to let them have you over. From then on I always had an inkling you were capable of something like this. Capable of anything.

—You are so full of shit.

—Thomas, you want to attribute your behavior to a set of external factors. You want to cede your life and decisions and consequences to forces outside of you, but that's the coward's way. And blaming your mother? It's so easy. You were not a lump of clay I molded. You and every other child comes into the world with their personality baked in. How else do you think a kid like Jim Avila is gay and designs dresses when his parents are white-trash farmers? The thing you always had was a need to blame. You get a bad grade, it's because the teacher doesn't like you. Some girl doesn't like you and it's because she's a slut or whatever else. I mean, as a mother I was exasperated by all this. I wanted to be on your side but there were too many battles. You were at war every day, and it was exhausting.

—So you take no responsibility.

—I take the same amount of responsibility as any parent. Which should be limited. If you were raised in a standard two-parent family, with all the money and stability in the world, you would have turned out exactly the same. Maybe with some superficial differences. You'd have slightly different clothes.

—That's an incredible statement.

—Thomas, I wasn't one of those mothers who waited ten years to have a child. I wasn't placing all my worldly hopes on the outcome of my womb.

—Wait. What's that got to do with anything? What does that even mean?

—It means I wasn't so awed by the idea of having a child that I went dancing around you like you were some golden calf. Most parents are so grateful to their children for existing that they become obsequious. I promised myself I would not be one of those obsequious mothers.

—Obsequious? You are amazing.

—I find all that disgusting. It begins a lifetime of perceived debt that does no one any good.

—I have no idea what you're talking about.

—Thomas, I did not think you some miracle bestowed upon me. You were born and I was happy to have you. And I don't think you thought of me as some miracle, either. We were, or should have been, partners. I was happy you existed and wanted you to thrive. My hope was that you were happy to exist and that you yourself would endeavor to thrive. But instead you were aggrieved by your existence and my role in it. I think that's why you were so drawn to Christ.

—I wasn't drawn to Christ. What does that mean?

—You used to draw the crucifix on your notebooks. Other kids were drawing spaceships or Grateful Dead skulls or penises, but you were drawing crucifixes. You thought that was you, suffering on the cross. I considered you a partner and an equal but you wanted to be beneath me and a martyr.

—You're the one who brought me to church.

—I brought you once. You know how I hate Christianity and all that wretched iconography. You know what? You see pictures of Buddha and he's sitting, reclining, at peace. The Hindus have their twelve-armed elephant god, who also seems so content but not powerless. But leave it to the Christians to have a dead and bloody man nailed to a cross. You walk into a church and you see a helpless man bleeding all over himself—how can we come away hopeful after such a sight? People bring their children to mass and have them stare for two hours at a man hammered to a beam and picked at by crows. How is that elevating? It's all about accountability for them.

—What is?

—The Christians, the Bible. It's all about who's at fault. A whole religion based on accountability. Who's to blame? What's the judgment? Who gets punished? Who gets jailed, banished, killed, drowned, decimated. You want to know the main takeaway most people got from Jesus's death? Not sacrifice, nothing like that. The takeaway, after all that Old Testament judgment, is that the Jews did it.

—Incredible.

—You loved it, though. Especially as a teenager. Young men love martyrdom. You get to be the victim and the hero at the same time. Do you remember when you said you wanted to be a priest?

—I didn't want to be a priest.

—A monk? What was it? It was Don's influence. Wasn't his mom some Bible thumper?

—She wasn't a Bible thumper.

—Don thought himself some kind of elevated young man, didn't he? He took himself very seriously. The last time I saw him he was spouting some very pious stuff. He looked at me like I was one of his parishioners, like he was taking an interest in me—that he might save me.

—You're faulting him for caring about you. I know how foreign that is to you. To care about someone. To care about their well-being.

—You mean me with you? If anything, I was too protective.

—Holy shit.

—What are you doing now? Don't get so excited. Stop the jumping around, Thomas. Please. I didn't make you get jobs. I allowed you to flounder. It made you soft. I let you quit college. I let you live at home.

—So why did you?

—I felt guilty. You guilted me into it. You made me feel like I'd done all these horrible things, so I coddled you. You'd have been better off in military school. The Army straightens boys like you out. You needed some discipline. You needed to be around people who wake up in the morning and go to work, do something.

—You didn't keep me safe.

—I did keep you safe.

—Whether or not you felt responsible for my birth, you're supposed to keep your children safe.

—I did as much as I could. As anyone could.

—You know what Mr. Hansen did with us? He played a game called "tailor." It involved him measuring various parts of our bodies.

—Did he undress you?

—He says he didn't.

—Do *you* remember him undressing you?

—No. But I could have buried that memory. We all could have.

—Oh get serious. So he took a tape measure or what?

—He put the tape measure against the insides of our legs. He did that to every kid, alone in his closet, and then we'd all lie on the bed together watching movies. He was breathing heavily the whole time.

—And that's what has you thinking your life is irreparable?

—No. It's just one of the many things I shouldn't have seen or had to endure. Things I wouldn't have been subjected to if you were present and sober.

—Thomas. I remember very clearly sending you to Mr. Hansen's house. I was sober then and I'm sober now. It seemed like a fine idea, and a safe idea. There were kids going off on overnights all the time. Boy Scout trips, sports trips, band trips. Summer camp. It was not an outrageous proposition to allow a group of boys to sleep at a trusted adult's house. And now you tell me that this man put a tape measure against your leg, and that this is the great crime of the world.

—I didn't say that.

—Thomas, why don't you kidnap some kid born with leukemia, or a woman who's been sold into prostitution? You had a tape measure against your leg and it's paralyzed you for life.

—I can't stand you.

—Fine. But someone needs to give you some tough love. You're soft. You need to find some steel.

—And *you're* the embodiment of inner strength? Let me enumerate the places I found you blacked out. In the backyard. In your car, in the garage, as if you meant to kill yourself with carbon monoxide and fell asleep in the middle of the task. And growing up, I found you in my bed. That was once a week, at least, you'd be in my bed. I could smell the wine fermenting. You know that smell? It's this musty animal smell, like your body was some wet sponge full of everything it wiped off the dinner dishes. See, the nice thing about having you here is that I can see what sort of withdrawal you go through. Are you already jonesing?

—No, I am not. I'm not the person you're battling. You're battling me from fifteen years ago. I have everything under control and I think you know that. You're fighting the former, lesser version of myself—so why bother?

—You know, only a narcissist could come up with a phrase like that. "Former, lesser version of myself." That's evidence of someone who's spent a lot of time thinking about herself, perfecting certain phrases. You know what? I just had an idea. I think, after I let the other people go, I'll hold on to you. You'll get clean, and I'll have more time to get some things cleared up.

—You'll be caught within twenty-four hours. Tommy, please, let us all go. I know we can start again. I want you alive. I don't want to see you killed out here, but I have a terrible feeling that's where all this is heading.

—You know what, Mom? I'm done with you tonight. The sun's

coming up and I'm tired, and when I'm this tired, I can't listen to you spout your nonsense. I don't even know if you're on something now, so I'm going to leave you for tonight. And tomorrow we'll have more fun like we've had tonight. Maybe you'll be clearer in the head, and you'll have given some thought to your culpability in all this. Okay?

—Thomas, stop. You can't leave me like this.

—You'll be fine.

—Thomas.

—Nighty night.

BUILDING 52

—You're back.

—You hungry?

—With all these granola bars? How could I be hungry?

—I'm giving you most of the food, Kev, because you were the first. But now that there are four of you, I have to be careful divvying up what's left.

—Four people?

—I guess I didn't tell you that already.

—You have four people out here?

—It wasn't even that hard, after you. I admit the others weren't, you know, military men. And my mom was easy.

—You have your mom here?

—There were a lot of things we needed to talk about.

—Makes sense.

—I know it does.

—You're a family man.

—I don't need the sarcasm, Kev. This is all lining up. It's working so fluidly that I know it was meant to be. And I have to thank you. You made it all possible.

—At least until they come and shoot you, which will be momentarily.

—You know Kev, I don't know if that's true. It's been three days so far, and I don't see or hear any sign of anyone coming. To me this is actually a sign of how far astronauts have slipped in our collective national esteem. You think Neil Armstrong would have been allowed to rot on a military base like this for two, three days? There would have been an international manhunt.

—You know, I don't know if I need to talk to you anymore. It's a waste of breath. Any minute, you'll see a shadow in the trees, and that'll be the sniper shooting you dead.

—Kev, that's a very vivid and very graphic picture. You're a military man, so I assume you probably get off on that kind of thing, picturing bullets ripping through skulls and flesh. But I can't let it bother me. Today is a good day.

—You're getting sicker.

—No, Kev, I'm getting better. I got some sleep last night, and then what happened this morning—it means that everything's brightening for me, more so every day. The answers I'm getting are very helpful, first of all. And the craziest and best thing just happened to me while I was walking on the beach this morning. I saw a woman and I believe it's a sign of good things to come.

—You saw a woman?

—I did. I know this park is closed and the shoreline should be empty, but this morning, before you woke up, I was down by the bluffs overlooking the ocean, and it was high tide, so I was deciding if I should risk going down to the beach. I was just standing there when I saw this figure along the shore. Seeing anyone at all freaked me out, so I dove onto the ground, thinking it might be someone looking for you or the congressman or something. So I was crouched down in the grass, and when I looked up the figure was closer and I could see it was a woman. A woman and her dog. I kept watching her as she came closer, and pretty soon I could make out that she had this cable-knit sweater on, and jeans rolled up to her calves, and she was barefoot and was throwing this tennis ball into the surf where her dog would retrieve it. The sun was still low, and everything was golden, and I thought I was seeing my destiny.

—I can't believe I have to listen to this.

—I mean, this was the woman of my dreams, Kev! Just beyond my wildest fantasies. And for an instant I thought that I could get to her. You know, run down to the beach and unite with her. But then I realized that I couldn't. I couldn't talk to her, because I had you here, and I was hating myself for that, for taking you and preventing any chance with her, and then I was laughing at myself, because I've never been within a hundred miles of a woman like that, never had a shot at anyone like her, so who was I kidding? I've never been within reach of anyone I coveted. But I have to thank you, Kev, because if it wasn't for you, I wouldn't be here, and I wouldn't have seen her.

—I think you should talk to her. Now. She might still be there.

—Wait, what? That was a pretty dramatic change in tone. Oh, I get it. You want me to talk to her so she can wonder who I am, why I'm here, maybe report me to the local police, maybe express some vague concern about the man staying at the closed Army base. And that's why I can't talk to her. I'm smarter than that, Kev! But shit, on the other hand, it must be a sign, right?

—It has to be a sign.

—It does, right? Why would a woman like that, who in every way fits the description I've had in my head since I was ten, be walking alone on this deserted beach? Where did she come from?

—She's looking for you, Thomas.

—Don't patronize me.

—I believe in destiny, Thomas. That's how I met my wife. We shouldn't have met at all. I missed a plane, ended up seated next to her in the airport lobby, and that was that. I believe in true love, and destiny, and love at first sight. And I think you have all three happening right there on the beach now. So you're a fool if you don't pursue it.

—Shit. This is so tough.

—It's easy. Easiest thing in the world. Go for it.

—I have to, right?

—You do.

—Damn. I'm stuck, though.

—You have to act, dude. You have to talk to her. How far could she have gone? Go get her. This is the scene in the movie when the guy goes after the woman he's meant to be with. Go.

—You think I should?

—I do.

—Fuck. Maybe this is what this was all about. You, the congressman, my mom, Hansen, maybe it was all meant to lead me to this woman in the sweater.

—It's the only logical answer.

BUILDING 52

—You're back already. No luck?

—No. No sign of her at all.

—But later today. You've got to look for her then.

—Why?

—If she's walking her dog now, she's got to be walking it in the afternoon, too.

—I've never had a dog. You walk them twice a day?

—At least, man. At least twice a day. So you've got to stay on watch. She'll be out there again for sure.

—Okay.

—You already missed one opportunity. The universe was telling you to go after her this morning.

—Shit. Okay, I will. I will. I probably have what, two days left, max.

—Tops. All the more reason to go after her.

—Okay, thanks.

—No problem.

—I'm really sorry you're chained like this.

—You want to let me loose? I can help you with whatever.

—No. You know I can't.

—Thomas. We're friends.

—I know, I know.

—I can watch things here when you're on the beach. I can do whatever. We're in this together now.

—No. I shouldn't.

—You should.

—I shouldn't. It's not that I don't trust you.

—You do, right?

—Absolutely. But think of it—if you go around helping me, you'll be complicit. I can't have that. I need you to stay innocent.

—Thomas.

—No. I know I'm right. I'll see you soon.

BUILDING 55

—You awake?

—No.

—Mom. Wake up.

—Oh Thomas.

—Why are you sleeping? It's three in the afternoon.

—I'm in pain. Thomas, you have to let me go. I'm in such pain.

—That's just withdrawal.

—Withdrawal from what, you fool?

—How would I know?

—I'm not on anything, Thomas. But I am sixty-two years old. And being chained up like this is very hard on my body. Have you seen my leg?

—It's ugly, but that's just because you're leaning on it funny. If you just laid your leg down like everyone else it wouldn't turn all purple. Jesus. That is disgusting.

—You have to unshackle me, Thomas.

—I can't. Just lay your leg down, and it'll take the pressure off. Give it an hour.

—I can't believe you.

—I just came in to tell you that this was all happening for a reason.

—That's what you've been saying.

—No. I mean that I think there's a more divine purpose.

—Oh no.

—I saw a vision this morning and I think it's a sign. I mean, here I am in the middle of nowhere, and you're here, and the astronaut is here and the congressman, and then I see this woman who has been in my dreams since I was ten or so. It all has to mean something.

—Thomas, you brought us all here. This is no coincidence.

—Right, but that was just a prelude to this woman on the beach. She was wearing exactly what I always saw her wearing in my visions, jeans and a cable-knit sweater. And there she was, alone on the beach with her dog. And now I feel like I'm so close to something. Once I talk to her, she'll know who I am and why we were on the beach at the same time.

—And what? You go skipping down the coast and fall in love? Or you bring her back here to show her what you've done? She'll want to be with a kidnapper? She'll fall for you and your wonderful achievement here? You're nuts, I know this, but you're not *this* nuts, are you?

—This is the problem with you. You've never had any kind of

optimism. You're such a dark-hearted cynic. You pretend like you have these New Age ideas about things, and every so often you have some experience you think is magical or whatever, but really you're a very very pessimistic, black-hearted person. So you can't even conceive of something like this happening. Something pure and good, like a woman appearing on the beach for me. You don't believe in anything clicking into place. Your life has been a sloppy mess so you assume mine will be, too. You don't believe in destiny.

—Well, Thomas, I actually do. I believe you are destined to go to jail, and be evaluated by a clinical psychologist if you're lucky. And they'll determine that you have delusions of grandeur, and display acute antisocial behavior, and have monumental control issues, and you think destiny is seeing a woman on the beach during a suicidal kidnapping escapade.

—Good. That's good.

—It's not good. None of this is good.

—You know what's telling? The astronaut, who I barely know, is more supportive of me pursuing this woman than you are.

—Because he wants you *caught,* you imbecile. Of *course* he wants you making contact with some woman on the beach. He wants her to report you.

—On the surface, sure, that might seem true. But you know what? Kev actually cares. You know that he and I were friends in college, right?

—Of course you were.

—How would you know? We were. That's why he's out here. He confided in me when we were in school, he told me he wanted to go up in the Space Shuttle, and now it's fifteen years later for him and now there's no chance that will ever happen. So I'm trying to help him see a new path, and he's appreciative of me.

—I'm sure he is, Thomas.

—And he met his wife in a similar way that I met this woman.

—While kidnapping his mother and locking her to a pole.

—No! No. No. Why do you have to be so cynical? Don't you see that something extraordinary is happening?

—Thomas, I think you are very very ill.

—

—Where are you going?

BUILDING 52

—Back already! You see her?

—I saw her, but not the right her. Tell me something, Kev: Your parents were probably perfect?

—They were not. They got divorced and both remarried.

—But they're probably all best friends. You all have Thanksgivings together.

—No, we do not. No one likes anyone else.

—But that's recent. Growing up?

—I had eleven different bedrooms before I was in high school. I was beaten repeatedly by my father, and he once broke my arm on purpose.

—This sounds rehearsed. You've said this before.

—I keep it foremost in my mind.

—But still you succeed.

—Yes. Not the answer you wanted?

—I don't know.

—You been back to the beach?

—Not yet.

—You should get out there. You never know. You definitely don't want to miss the girl while you're talking to me.

—Yeah.

—You should go.

—I know. I know. Thanks Kev. I feel good about this.

BUILDING 52

—Kev!

—Oh hey.

—You were napping?

—Well, buddy, there's not much else to do out here. You've been running? You're out of breath.

—I ran back here. I had to tell you. I met her.

—You met the girl?

—I did.

—Wow. Good. I'm so glad.

—I know. I did like you said. I went back to the bluff, and I waited for her to come by again with her dog. It was three hours or so, but she came back. About five o'clock.

—See, told you.

—Yeah, so I saw her down the beach, and she was walking toward where I was, but there wasn't any way for me to get down there. I hadn't figured out a route to the beach. And the bluff there is too steep to jump or shimmy down. So I start freaking out, looking around for some path or something. But I had to find one quick, so I could get down to the beach and start walking toward her like it's casual, like I'm just like her, someone who walks the beach this time every day, right?

—Right. You're smooth.

—So I run about a quarter mile down the way, away from her, and finally I find this huge path down to the shore. It must have been some kind of boat launch back in the day. So I get down to the beach and can still see her down the way, walking toward me. And you know what the great thing is?

—It all sounds great.

—She's wearing the same sweater, this cream cable-knit sweater. I mean, the sweater is half the whole thing for me. Any woman who wears a sweater like that knows everything I want. And the jeans rolled up. I mean, a barefoot woman with jeans and a white cable-knit sweater! That's my fantasy.

—And it should be. So you talked to her or what?

—Well, that was cool. I mean, I'm not ever good at approaching any woman, but she made it easy. The first thing she did was wave. I mean, just when we were in clear sight of each other, but still pretty far away, she waved. We were the only two people for miles, so I guess it's not unnatural to wave, but still. She made the first move.

—A clear sign.

—It is, right? We're all alone out there, and the sun's dropping over the water, and she's throwing this ball to her dog, and there we are, walking toward each other. It was like we were the last two people on Earth.

—Or the first.

—Right. It was beautiful.

—And then?

—Well, eventually we get close enough to talk, and we say hello, and I ask what kind of dog she's got, and she says it's some kind of Labradoodle, which itself is another sign, given I'm allergic and that's a hypoallergenic dog.

—And you told her this?

—I told her I was allergic. Not that it was a sign that we were destined for each other. I'm not nuts.

—And she looked like . . .

—Oh god. I mean, perfection. She's a little younger than me, I think, probably thirty, but honestly, she's the embodiment of everything I've ever wanted. She's got the clothes, I knew that, but then she has this great J.Crew face, you know, no makeup, just this handsome face, these small blue eyes, a little crinkly around the eyes, like she's been outside a lot and doesn't care about a few wrinkles. I like that.

—Body is good?

—Like an athlete. I didn't ask her yet, but I bet she played soccer or lacrosse or something like that. She's a little short, so one of those sports where you can be smaller and fast.

—So you found out where she lives?

—Apparently there's a small town just at the edge of the park. She's a vet there. Isn't that incredible? I guess she's the only one for twenty miles or something. And she walks about five miles a day with

her dog, who she says needs long walks twice a day or else he chews
up the house.

—Told you. Twice a day.

—Right. And this is just about the endpoint of her walk. So
again, a perfect sign that she was meant to be here, and I was meant to
be here. Think of it: if I had been half a mile farther down the beach,
I never would have seen her. If I hadn't brought you or anyone here, I
wouldn't be here. Actually, if I'd only brought you here, and if I'd left
after a few days, I wouldn't have seen her at all. So it was destiny that
I kept taking people, because this is three days in, and I only saw her
now. It all connects. Everything was necessary.

—And did she ask why you were here?

—Her dog liked me, too.

—That's good. Why wouldn't he?

—Yeah, right? I told her I was just a tourist, just checking out
Fort Ord, taking pictures. She did bring up the fact that the park is
closed, but I think I scored some points by saying I just went around
the barrier with my van and had been camping here.

—And did you bring her back up here? I mean, where is she?

—No, no. I didn't think that was the way to do it. Do you?

—I don't know. Carpe diem, right?

—C'mon. You know I'm not that stupid. I bring her up here, one
of you guys sees her, starts yelling, everything turns to shit.

—Sure, but don't you want to talk to her? Sit somewhere?

—There's no way I can bring her here.

—So what did you say? How'd you leave it?

—I just said I'd see her again tomorrow.

—Okay.

—And see, that's where things got interesting. I feel pretty proud of myself here, because I knew she walks in the morning, too, right? But I thought if I told her I knew that, it might scare her. So I couldn't say, "Hey, I saw you this morning, too."

—Right. You don't want her to think you're strange.

—Exactly. But I didn't want to have to wait till tomorrow afternoon to see her again. So I needed her to volunteer the information that she does a morning walk, too.

—And did she?

—She did indeed. When I said, all casual, "Well, maybe I'll see you tomorrow afternoon," she said, "Oh, I'll be back before then. I walk in the morning, too."

—Perfect.

—Right. So I'm set.

—Wow. This is incredible. You're so close.

—I know.

—And tomorrow, what happens? You bring her up here? I don't mean so close that she can see us, but up here in general?

—I don't know. Damn. I can't.

—Why not? You need someplace to close the deal, don't you?

—Close the deal?

—I don't mean you're gonna make babies. But it seems like you walk up here, find a warm and quiet nook where you can at least get a first kiss or something.

—Yeah. Right.

—There's no other way. This is how you know if she really digs you. It's always a change of venue. You know how I told you about meeting my future wife?

—You were at the airport?

—We both missed our flights, and we started talking just there in the waiting area. But then I asked her to get some food and a drink with me. Just in the airport bar, like twenty feet away, but that little trip, those twenty feet, meant everything. It meant that she liked me enough to stay in the airport when she could have gone home. And to walk with me, from one place to another, to have a drink with me, a stranger. That's the sign she's intrigued enough to take a chance. But until the woman does that, follows you somewhere, you'll never know.

—Right.

—Damned straight I'm right. So tomorrow, you talk to her, you see if she'll come up here. Just look around the fort. If it's meant to be, she comes up, no problem. She's already out on a walk. You make some excuse, like you have a fire up here you need to feed. Something to get you off the beach and up the hill.

—Brilliant. Thanks, Kev.

—No problem.

—You know, I told my mom about all this, about you helping me out here, and how far back we go, and she was such a bitch about it. She doesn't believe we're friends, that I could know someone like you.

—Who cares what she thinks? She doesn't understand.

—Not even close, right? Jesus, I'm wired.

—So what'll you do the rest of the night?

—I don't know. But I feel like I can will anything to happen.

—You're in the zone.

—Shit, I did have this one idea. I thought it was outside my reach completely, but now I'm not so sure.

—What is it?

—I shouldn't say. It wouldn't happen. Even thinking it is pretty illegal.

—Thomas, you're unstoppable. You never know. Like you said, things are happening for you. What was the idea?

—Well, I thought of going back to Marview and getting a cop.

—A cop? Like a police officer?

—Yeah. It's stupid I know.

—And then bring him here?

—Yeah. Is that nuts?

—You wouldn't hurt him?

—I haven't hurt anyone.

—Then I think you should give it a shot.

—Really? I don't think I can pull it off.

—What? You got *me*, right? How much harder could a cop be?

—You weren't armed.

—Thomas, this is your time. This is all the coal of your life compressed into a diamond.

—Maybe I get an older cop.

—Take your pick. You're unstoppable. You might be invincible.

—I'll find the right one.

—There you go.

—I'll bring him back.

—It'll be a cinch.

—Wish me luck.

—Good luck, Thomas.

BUILDING 57

—Wow, this is the greatest week of my life.

—

—Sorry. You probably don't understand that.

—

—Okay, comparatively, it's not such a good week for you. You've been, well, I guess you've been brought here. I just mean that bringing an astronaut here was hard, but getting an actual cop here . . . Jesus. Kev said I was invincible and now I know it's true. Shit, I forgot to tell him. I'll be back.

BUILDING 52

—You were right, my man.

—

—Kev? You asleep?

—What's that?

—It's me.

—You're back?

—I am. And I got one.

—You got what?

—A cop, man. Just like you said. And he was easier than you.

—Oh shit.

—What?

—You brought him here?

—He's two buildings over.

—Unharmed?

—He's fine.

—And you weren't followed?

—Nothing. He was alone. I left his phone right there on the street.

—Oh Jesus.

—What? It's true. I'm unstoppable. You were right.

—He's okay?

—He's fine. What are you worried about?

—I don't know. What do you plan to do with him?

—I don't know. I mean, I know generally. I have some general police-work questions. Just some stuff I wanted to talk about. He doesn't look like he'd know a whole lot.

—What time is it?

—About ten. It took me an hour to get there, and then a couple hours to stake out the scene. He was standing outside some party like a valet.

—I can't believe you took a cop.

—You made me believe it was possible, Kev. I have to thank you for that.

BUILDING 57

—You don't look very good. Maybe I used too much on you. It's just chloroform. You won't die.

  —What is this? Where am I?

  —You're safe. And you're far from anyone hearing you but me. I have four others out here and everyone's safe. No one will be hurt, even you. We've been here for three days. I am a moral man and a principled man and I might be invincible. Do you understand that?

  —What's your plan, buddy?

  —Say what?

  —Tell me your plan. Is this some kind of shakedown or something?

  —A shakedown?

  —You trying to get back at me for giving you a ticket or busting you for drugs or whatever?

—You know, I don't like you much so far. You've got an abrasive personality. I watched you half the night, just to see if you looked like a hardass, but you looked more like a dentist. A dentist dressed like a cop.

—

—With the others I've apologized first and foremost for having to bring them here under these circumstances, but I don't know how sorry I am about you. I've had some bad experiences with your kind.
—My kind?
—Cops. But at the same time, I've had plenty of good experiences, too. I want you guys to be good. I want to believe you want to do the right thing. But too often you fuck that up.

—

—I forgot to tell you that you're here to talk. That's why you're here. I ask some questions and you answer them, okay?
—Why?
—Why? Because I have you handcuffed and I say so. You must be familiar with the rules of a deposition, right?
—You're calling this a deposition?
—It's as close to that as anything else. There are just some general questions I need answered. I don't know anything about you, but you were wearing the uniform so I figured you'd know some answers. I guess you could say I profiled you.

—

—You don't like that?

—

—And the sooner we're done the sooner I'm gone and you're free. Okay?

—Go to hell.

—You really are abrasive. I didn't expect that. You have such a friendly face. You remind me of some mailman or TV dad. I picture you putting on a cardigan after work, opening the newspaper, helping your kids with their homework.

—

—Unless you're guarding some private party.

—

—Wow, that is the life, huh? A Monterey beat cop during the day, at night guarding private parties for time and a half. How long have you been a cop?

—

—You have to answer now.

—Twenty years.

—Twenty years. You ever take the detective test?

—Up yours.

—Ah. I take it the answer is yes. What are you looking for? Some ship you're planning to signal? There's no one out the window. Are you that dumb? You're inside an abandoned military barracks and you're gonna signal some ship two miles into the Pacific?

—We're at Fort Ord.

—Good. You're the first one to guess. Were you a Marine or something? You're a very stoic guy.

—

—Okay. I guess I've had a streak of more talkative people, so I was getting spoiled there for a while. I didn't need to explain the rules. The rules are that you're here to talk to me and to answer my questions. I have a taser over there. I guess you already saw that. And I have other stuff outside that I could use if you're really being unco-operative. But I'm not a violent guy. I haven't harmed anyone. I have four others out here, and everyone is healthy and well fed. And I think I'm almost done finding out what I need to find out. So if you cooper-ate this could all be over soon enough.

—

—Maybe I picked the wrong cop. Listen, I had a night to waste until my destiny tomorrow, and I was just looking for someone from your department. I have nothing against you in particular. I knew there's no other way any of you guys would sit down to talk to me. You get it? I've written letters to the department and never got an answer. I asked to talk to anyone and no one could bother.

—

—So anyway. Now that you're here, here's the plan. You talk to me, you answer questions, and we'll be fine. If you don't, then I tase you. I mace you. I do stuff like that. Stuff you've probably done to people all the time. You'll find it familiar. And the sooner you talk to me and we get finished, the sooner you can get free. Does all that make sense?

—Yes.

—Huh. That was almost sudden. Suddenly you're talking. Have you done this kind of thing before?

—No.

—But is it part of your training or anything? Do you have a simu-lation for this kind of situation? Being chained to a post and being asked questions? I guess this is sort of a hostage thing.

—I assume you had a bad run-in with a cop?

—We're not talking about me right now. I want you to talk about you. I can't sleep, and it's hours till dawn, so we're going to talk. We're going to go through a little biographical portrait of you. I want to understand you and your kind. You were born where?

—Modesto.

—Modesto! Wow. Okay, Modesto. Two parents?

—Yes.

—Dad was a cop?

—Mom.

—Mom was a cop! Wow. That is fantastic. And Dad did what?

—He designed furniture.

—He designed furniture? He designed furniture? That is the best thing I've heard all week. I swear to god. Wow. He designed furniture! Your mom went out with her gun and everything, and your dad made her breakfast and then stayed home drawing little pictures of ottomans?

—

—Sorry. I didn't mean any disrespect. Sorry. Your dad drew awesome pictures of ottomans. Not little pictures. Big ones! Manly ones.

—Where is this going?

—So you become a cop why? To follow in Mom's footsteps? You know, I'm thinking things were complicated in your house. Maybe Dad's feeling emasculated given Mom makes more money. Did he work at home?

—

—He did! In a way, he was a homemaker, wasn't he?

—

—Sorry. I shouldn't take cheap shots. So you become a cop why? Because you want to do good?

—You don't really have a cop look. That's why I took you. You seemed more harmless than the other options. You ever have a mustache, goatee, that kind of thing?

—

—No answer? Is that classified information? Cop facial hair choices are classified? Did you just smile? I made you laugh. That is awesome. Now we're best friends. Okay, let's back up. Now that we're besties I need to know everything. I'm assuming public school?

—

—Don't go shy now. I'm worked up. You don't want me getting that taser. I'm more likely to use it when I'm excited. So: public school? Don't nod. I need answers. It's dark and nodding doesn't work when it's dark. As you can imagine, I can't turn lights on or maybe those ships you think you were signaling might actually see us.

—Yes. Public school.

—Okay. College?

—Two years.

—Where?

—Chico State.

—Chico State. Chico State. Okay. I can see that. Then what? You drop out?

—I ran out of money.

—Were you planning to become a cop at that point?

—I don't know.

—You were studying what?

—Theater.

—Theater! Theater! Oh shit. That is fantastic. Your dad's a

furniture designer, and you're studying theater. And Mom was what kind of cop, by the way? Like a clerk or actually driving around in a cruiser?

—Driving around. Patrol. Then she was a sergeant.

—Wow. Okay. So Frank wants to be what, an actor? You were wanting to be an actor?

—I don't know. I did everything—set design, props, directing.

—Frank, I really like you now. You look like the *Family Ties* dad and you studied theater at Chico State. I like you. So I'm hoping I don't have to dislike you later. So then you drop out of college, and then what?

—I worked.

—Doing?

—Telemarketing.

—Oh shit. That's terrible. Were you good at it?

—No.

—Selling what?

—Home security systems.

—Okay. For how long?

—A year.

—And then what? Then the police academy?

—No, then Europe.

—You went to Europe? Like backpacking, Eurail pass, all that?

—Yes.

—Frank, I can't tell you how much I love that. You are awesome. I have to say, I'm so encouraged that there are cops who studied theater at Chico State and then went backpacking through Europe. You should get the word out about that! You know the perception is that you cops are a bunch of gorillas who never left the state, don't you? They should put guys like you out there more, do some community events, that kind of thing. All you guys stay in your cars and never talk to anyone. You know what a problem that is for your PR? They should have a Meet Frank the Cop Night, where you talk to people about your crazy adventures in Greece and shit. Isn't that a great idea?

—I don't know.

—It is! And I'm assuming you went to Greece?

—I did.

—Rented a scooter, rode it drunk, picked up English girls?

—More or less.

—You know, in another life we would have almost been friends. You seem okay. I'm glad I took you. You married?

—

—C'mon, I'm not going to harm your wife. And if I wanted to, I could anyway. I could find out in a second whether or not you're married. I know your name.

—Go ahead, call the station and ask.

—Look at you! You're clever. You want me to call the station. Then you yell out or something, they trace the call, they get the coordinates from the cell phone company, and we're found. That's clever. Well, it's almost clever. It's not really all that clever. You couldn't be all that clever and be working for the Marview police. And where I picked you up, what was that? You're guarding some private residence or something?

—I was providing security at an event.

—You ever shoot anyone?

—At a private party?

—No. Funny, though. Have you?

—No.

—Did you ever shoot your gun?

—On duty?

—Yes on duty.

—I've fired my sidearm three times on duty.

—Three times. Who were the three targets?

—One was a man who had robbed a dry cleaner's.

—Was he armed?

—Yes, I believe he was.

—"Yes I believe he was." You know, you just set yourself back a hundred years. That is precisely the kind of bullshit answer people expect from cops, and here you're giving it to me. So did he get away?

—He was armed, and he did get away. He ran across a four-lane highway and got into a car.

—You fired at him and missed.

—I have to assume I missed.

—Okay, who else?

—Once at an animal.

—What kind of animal?

—A dog.

—A dog.

—Yes.

—So you're saying that one of the three times you shot your gun was at a dog?

—Yes.

—That is fascinating. That really means you're telling me the truth. Because if you were hiding anything from me you wouldn't mention that. And you're also trying to humanize yourself. You've read the handbook. Humanize yourself, talk about your allergies, weaknesses, family, frailties, and maybe the kidnapper will spare you. That about right?

—

—So did you hit the dog?

—No I did not.

—You're a bad shot or what?

—I'm a decent shot.

—But you missed the dry cleaning man and the dog.

—Both encounters were in the evening and both targets were moving quickly.

—Are you nearsighted or anything?

—No.

—So who was the third target of your gun?

—He was just a man. Disturbed man.

—How old?

—Thirty or so, I think.

—Wait. What? He was thirty? What was his name?

—I don't know. It was a bunch of consonants.

—What do you mean? Where was this?

—Here. Marview.

—What? Why were you here?

—I used to work here. I was transferred after.

—What was his name?

—It was a foreign name.

—Foreign like from where?

—I think it was Vietnam.

—What?

—Vietnamese. I think it was.

—What was his name?

—I don't know. It started with *B*.

—The last name started with *B*?

—Yes. I know that.

—And his first name?

—It was American.

—Was it Don?

—It could be.

—Was it Don Banh?

—I don't know. Did you know him?

—Now you're lying. Now you think I'll kill you because you killed my friend. Did you kill Don Banh?

—No.

—You said you shot him.

—We shouldn't talk about this now.

—We have to talk about this now. Did you shoot Don Banh?

—

—You better talk.

—I didn't kill him. My shot didn't kill him.

—Fuck. Fuck. I didn't think I'd actually get one of you guys who was actually there. You're saying you were actually one of the cops that night?

—I don't know.

—I will kill you if you don't talk. Do you hear me? I will kill you. I will tase you till you die. I'll think of other ways. I'll take a rock and break your head open.

—I can't tell you anything if you're planning to kill me.

—Your only chance is talking to me. If you don't, I kill you. I haven't threatened anyone else this way but you I will kill. I thought I just picked up some random cop but now it's you, one of you from that night. So we need to start talking.

—Okay.

—Fuck. Wait. I need to get away from you for a second.

BUILDING 53

—Congressman?

—

—Congressman?

—

—Sorry. I know it's the middle of the night. It's two a.m. I need your help here.

—Thomas.

—Would you think less of me if I did something to a cop?

—A cop?

—I have one a few buildings over.

—A cop? Son, don't do anything to him. Don't harm that man. How the hell did you get a cop out here?

—He was just guarding some party. He was alone.

—Kid, you need to stop all this now. You will be dead by sunup.

—I don't think so. I'm fairly sure I'm being shielded by some divine force. Some kind of light is protecting me and allowing me to get through all this. So I think I have some time. I dumped his phone. There's no chance anyone knows where he is. Where any of us are. And this guy killed my friend.

—Okay. I don't know if you know this for sure, but I guarantee you harming him will not bring you comfort in any way. It's comfort you're after, correct?

—I don't know.

—Peace of mind?

—Okay. Peace of mind.

—You think harming a police officer will bring you peace of mind? You think you'll sleep better at night after harming a police officer?

—I don't know.

—I assure you there's no chance. You will never sleep again. If you want to talk to him, talk to him. Find out what you want to find out. The truth will bring you some peace. I can just about guarantee it. You say you're a moral man?

—I am a moral man.

—Then prove it. If this man harmed your friend then ask him about it. Seek your truth. But you have to be better than the violence. Exalt yourself, son.

—Okay.

—And afterward I have an idea how you can end all this without any harm coming to you. I've been thinking of a plan for you. You say your mother's here, right?

—Wait. Not now. I'll be back.

BUILDING 57

—So you know his name was Don Banh?

—

—What, now you're not talking?

—I don't think we should do this.

—This is the worst time to start testing me. They keep saying some sniper will kill me anyway. I might as well take you with me.

—It won't do any good to rehash this.

—That's not your decision to make. You're going to answer my questions like you've been doing. So what happened?

—He was armed and I fired at him.

—Were there other officers with you?

—Yes.

—Did they hit him?

—Yes they did.

—Did they kill him?

—Yes they did. Well, he died later at the hospital.

—Why did they shoot him?

—He was armed and was threatening officers.

—What was he armed with?

—A knife.

—Where was he?

—In his backyard, I believe.

—Okay. We're going to do this in a workmanlike way. You answer every single question I have or else I do something to you. As long as you answer the questions I can hold steady. But if you piss me off I won't be able to control it. Are you ready?

—Yes.

—So your shift starts at what time?

—Three in the afternoon.

—And it goes until?

—Eleven p.m.

—What happened at the beginning of the shift?

—Most of the night was typical. From three until eight, I was patrolling.

—And what other calls did you respond to?

—I don't remember all of them, but there were two calls about the same homeless person defecating in the Dollar Tree parking lot.

—And what happened there?

—I spoke to the gentleman, and told him he was not permitted to do that.

—You didn't arrest him.

—No. He was harmless.

—So you used restraint there.

—I always try to.

—Okay. I want to keep that statement in my back pocket for a little while. This concept of restraint is interesting to me. So what other calls were there that night?

—One or two instances of citizens seeing suspicious characters in their neighborhoods. That kind of thing.

—And what do you do in that situation?

—I drive over, look around, maybe wait with my lights off, see if I see anyone skulking about.

—And did you see anyone skulking about?

—No.

—Anything else?

—That night I believe there was someone bashing mailboxes.

—All right. Then what happens?

—Well, about eight fifteen p.m. we got a call about a man who had been acting erratically at the Denny's on the highway.

—What exactly did you hear?

—That a man in his early to mid thirties had come into a Denny's and had taken off his shirt. Then he'd gone into the kitchen and had put on an apron.

—That's it?

—Then he returned to the dining area and apparently stood on one of the tables. And then he walked from table to table that way. Standing on the tabletops, yelling.

—While wearing the apron.

—Yes.

—And that was the incident at Denny's? What was he yelling?

—He was yelling loudly about how there was a reckoning coming and how powerful he was. It was apocalyptic. He said he made the
world and could end it.

—Okay. And then what?

—I went to the Denny's to check it out, but he had left. I drove
along the highway but didn't see any sign of him. The patrons were
divided about whether or not he arrived by car. None of them had
seen him enter or leave in a car, so I had no vehicle or plate to follow. I
had the suspicion that he had simply parked far enough away that no
one saw him arrive or leave by car.

—So you circled the neighborhood or what?

—I took statements from the staff and patrons, and meanwhile
there was an APB out for this young man.

—An all-points bulletin.

—Yes.

—This was big news in Marview.

—It was cause for concern.

—But he hadn't harmed anyone.

—He had endangered the patrons by jumping from table to table.
And he had stolen from the restaurant.

—What did he steal? It was syrup, correct?

—Yes. It was not a high-value item, but it was theft, and it's our
job to look into any theft.

—So what's next? Was everyone looking for him?

—Yes. The three other squad cars on patrol began looking
for him.

—By what, triangulating the neighborhood?

—We were looking within a five-mile radius for any cars driving erratically, any men fitting his description, or for any irregularities in general.

—But this was a Friday night. I expect there would be dozens of young men acting like asses.

—Not exactly like this. When the man is alone, it's cause for more concern. A bunch of teenagers, or a bunch of guys in general, it's one thing. But a man alone, without a shirt, jumping around a Denny's and stealing syrup—it's cause for special concern.

—So you're looking for him, too?

—Yes, after I took statements at the restaurant, I began a search.

—Without any identifying characteristics.

—Well, I had a description of the young man. I knew he was Amerasian. And he left wearing an apron.

—You know no one says "Amerasian" anymore.

—Listen. I know these kids. I was in Vietnam for Christ's sake. We said *Amerasian* for years. I can't keep up with terminology.

—So you drive around looking for him.

—Yes.

—For how long?

—Forty-five minutes, an hour.

—Then what?

—Then we received a call from his mother.

—What did she say?

—That he had come home, ranting and raving, and that he'd left with a big knife.

—Did you go to the house?

—I didn't, but another officer did. He took her statement and shared that information with the other officers.

—So now you're looking for a young man in an apron, no shirt, and carrying a big knife.

—Yes. And he took her car, so now we knew he was driving a blue Honda Accord.

—But you didn't find it.

—No. Then we got a call from a young woman's house.

—You remember her name?

—No. It might have been Lily.

—Lily Dubuchet.

—Yes, I believe that was it.

—Who called?

—Her father called because the young man had been there. He'd broken the large window in the house. Apparently he heaved a cinder block through the picture window in the living room. When the family came to the window, he was breaking the windows on their cars.

—With what?

—A brick at first, then large stones he took from the driveway. Some kind of decorative stones that he was throwing through the windows and windshields of their cars.

—So the father called after he'd left?

—No, he was still there when the father called.

—Okay. I didn't know that part.

—So two squad cars turned around and headed to the house.

—Were you one of those cars?

—I was.

—And when you got there?

—The young man was gone. I stayed to take a statement, and the other officer went in the direction the young man was last seen.

—He was driving his mom's car.

—Yes. He left and sped down Willow, toward the highway.

—Did he threaten anyone at this young woman's house?

—I don't know.

—But you do know.

—You're asking if he directly threatened anyone?

—Yes.

—He broke a plate-glass window.

—And was anyone harmed?

—Glass splintered throughout the room. Everyone was struck by glass fragments.

—And that's it?

—As far as I recall.

—What about the knife?

—What about it?

—Did he threaten anyone with the knife at that house?

—Not that I recall.

—So he breaks some windows and then drives off.

—Yes.

—And you go in pursuit.

—Another officer went looking for his car.

—You stayed to get statements.

—I stayed for a few minutes.

—Until?

—Until I got word on the radio that he was back home.

—So he went from Lily's house back home.

—Yes, apparently.

—So you went there.

—Yes. Three squad cars arrived at about the same time.

—And then what?

—We approached the front door and the mother came out.

—And did what?

—She said that her son had entered the house and had gone into the basement and locked himself inside.

—Okay. So there are how many cops at this point?

—Four.

—Four cops. And there's one man in the basement.

—Yes.

—At this point are you aware of what size man he is?

—Yes. We knew at that point he was about five seven, 150 pounds.

—Not a large man.

—No.

—So you four officers, you do what?

—Well, first we went inside and knocked on the door to the basement.

—And?

—And he told us to go fuck ourselves.

—Did you try to open the door?

—It was locked and it wasn't procedure to break it down.

—Why not?

—Well, he was armed, and we didn't know at that point if he'd further armed himself. His mother said that he had been acting erratically and had pushed her against a wall. So we felt his behavior was unpredictable.

—So you called more cops?

—We called the Monterey Peninsula Regional Special Response Unit, yes.

—This is a SWAT team.

—Yes.

—Tell me about the decision to call them.

—Well, SWAT team officers are trained for hostage situations and—

—Were there hostages in the house?

—We weren't sure.

—But did you have any evidence to suggest he'd taken a hostage?

—Not hard evidence, no.

—Did you ask the mother if her son had somehow snuck a hostage into the house?

—No, we did not.

—Did she tell you that he might have? Did she see some other person in the house?

—No.

—So I don't know where you get the idea that he might have had a hostage.

—We have to prepare for any eventuality. I'm not saying that a hostage situation was foremost on our minds. But it was one of the possibilities. Hostages aren't a prerequisite for the participation of the SWAT team.

—Okay, so at this point, you're still standing by the basement door or what?

—No. At that point, we removed the mother from the home and fell back to the driveway.

—You fell back? Like this is some great battle. Jesus.

—

—You set up a perimeter or what?

—We did.

—But you're still thinking that the threat is one man—a small man with a knife, sitting in his basement.

—At that point we didn't know what he was armed with or what he was capable of. He'd done some very erratic things, including assaulting his mother.

—Was there evidence of an assault on his mother?

—He pushed her against a wall.

—Were there blood, cuts, bruises?

—No.

—So we have a man who pushed his mom against a wall.

—Yes. And he was armed with a knife.

—And did he threaten his mother with that knife?

—I can't recall. But if he assaults someone, and he's holding a knife, I have to assume that's assault with a deadly weapon.

—But he didn't assault her with the knife.

—He assaulted her and he was holding a knife.

—But did he threaten his mother with a knife?

—I can't really recall.

—You can't recall. Listen, you've been honest and forthright so far. You should stay that way. I know it's been a while since I reminded you of this, but you're chained to a post.

—I don't think he threatened her, no.

—Thank you. So how long until the SWAT team arrives?

—Twenty, twenty-five minutes.

—How many on the SWAT team?

—Ten.

—All men?

—All men at that point.

—And so they arrive. Then what?

—They spread out throughout the property.

—What, like on the roof, backyard, everything?

—I think there were probably two covering the front door, two on the back porch door, and two on each of the other exits.

—What were the other exits?

—There were two basement windows that could be opened. Two of the men saw him near one of the windows, so we kept them guarded.

—And at that point, did you tell him to come out or what?

—We told him that he needed to come out, hands up, and surrender.

—You're using a megaphone?

—Yes.

—And did he answer?

—He told us to fuck ourselves.

—That's it?

—That was it for a while.

—How long did the verbal exchange go on for?

—Forty minutes maybe. He only answered us a few times. We tried to call him, but he was not picking up his cell phone.

—So for forty minutes, you're talking to him intermittently. Did you have any reason to believe that he was arming himself in any new way?

—How do you mean?

—Did he ever say, "Now I have a grenade," or anything like that?

—No he did not.

—He didn't build himself a cannon or nuclear warhead?

—No.

—So you still think he's a guy with a knife, walking around his basement. And he's alone.

—Yes. But we don't know if he's armed himself further. The mother said that there was the possibility of him hiding a gun down there.

—Had she ever seen a gun on him?

—No.

—Did she have a gun in the house he might be using?

—I don't believe so.

—So you have no real reason to think he's acquired a gun somehow.

—No hard evidence, no.

—Then what happens?

—Well, at a certain point, I'd say an hour in, he said he was coming out through the front door.

—Okay.

—And so we sent more of our team to the front door.

—How many men at the front door at that point?

—I would say twelve officers.

—And were you there?

—I was.

—Okay. Eight SWAT team members at the front door, and you and three regular Marview cops?

—Yes.

—All right. And who's guarding the backyard at that point?

—Two SWAT team members.

—And then what happened?

—We wait at the front door for a few minutes, and we see no sign of him at the front door. Then one of the SWAT guys in the backyard says that he's just emerged from one of the basement windows.

—So the front-door thing was a ruse.

—That was our understanding.

—So he comes out the back window. And then what? Where was he going?

—He seemed to be trying to escape through the backyard. He was heading for the fence at the back of the yard. We had to assume he was going to hop the fence and make off into the neighbor's property. So the SWAT team member saw him and told him to halt.

—And did he?

—He did. He stopped, turned, and that's when the officer saw that he was still carrying the knife.

—The same knife.

—Yes.

—Remind me how big the knife is. What kind was it?

—It was an eight-inch kitchen knife.

—Like the kind you'd use to cut what, a steak?

—Yes, a steak, a turkey.

—Was the blade eight inches, or the whole knife was eight inches?

—I don't recall.

—Okay, we both know it was a regular steak knife. The kind you get at Outback. A little bigger than a normal one at the dinner table.

—I can't confirm that.

—Well, I can. It's a fact. So he's standing there, and he's holding the Outback steak knife.

—He was holding the knife and he would not relinquish it. The officers demanded he drop the knife, but he refused.

—And when did you come to the backyard?

—Almost immediately.

—How soon till all fourteen cops are in the backyard?

—Two stayed in the front yard.

—Okay. Twelve of you.

—Maybe twenty seconds.

—So twenty seconds after he emerges from the basement, all twelve of you are in the backyard with him. And he's holding the knife, and you're all yelling for him to drop the knife.

—That's correct.

—Where in the backyard was he standing?

—He stopped running near the back fence and had taken some steps back toward the house, so I'd say he was in the middle-back of the yard.

—Okay. And where are all you guys?

—We made a half circle around him.

—So there are twelve of you surrounding him, all of you with guns drawn?

—Yes.

—You're pointing what kind of gun at him?

—My service revolver.

—And the SWAT guys?

—Semiautomatics.

—So there are twelve guns pointed at him.

—Yes.

—And what's he doing at this point?

—At that point he was waving the knife around in a threatening manner.

—Like how, exactly? He's jabbing it toward people?

—Yes. He's jabbing, and he's yelling.

—What was he saying to you?

—Saying he was immortal, that he would cut our eyes out. That kind of thing.

—Hold on a second. I didn't know the part about being immortal. That wasn't in the police report. Tell me everything you can remember him saying.

—Well, there was the stuff about being immortal. He would say, "You know, you guys are just shades." He called us shades. He said he was the source of light, that he was the sun. He said he was the sun and he couldn't be killed.

—That's it?

—He told us to stay away or lose our eyes.

—He mostly threatened your eyes?

—Yes. That he'd cut out our eyes.

—Anything else?

—He also said he wrote the Bible. He quoted some line.

—What line?

—I don't remember. Something about missing fathers.

—Did he say he would kill you?

—I think he said he would live forever. That he was a prophet.

—Did he say he would kill you?

—Not that I can remember.

—Now how far away from him are you at this point?

—Me myself?

—Yes.

—Maybe twenty-five feet.

—Did you fear for your life?

—I felt in danger, yes.

—Let me back up a second. What were you wearing at that point?

—Just my uniform.

—No bulletproof vest?

—I was wearing a vest, yes.

—Okay. So you're wearing a bulletproof vest. Are the SWAT team members wearing vests, too?

—Yes.

—So all twelve of you were wearing vests?

—Yes.

—Okay. Would a bulletproof vest stop a knife?

—How do you mean?

—If I threw a knife from twenty-five feet away, would the vest stop it from penetrating your skin?

—Yes. I would think so.

—It can stop a bullet, right? So it could stop a kitchen knife.

—Yes.

—Okay. Were you wearing a helmet?

—I was not.

—But the SWAT guys were.

—Yes.

—So most of you are wearing helmets, and everyone's wearing vests. But you say you were concerned for your life.

—I was.

—Please explain that to me.

—We had an armed man who was in some kind of psychotic state. He attacked his mother and he was acting erratically, swinging around a large knife.

—But there's twelve guns against one knife. And with the vests, you're basically standing behind bulletproof glass.

—Vests are not like bulletproof glass. And remember, this man had legs. He could get to any one of us in a second or two.

—And that's what he tried to do?

—He was moving around. And for a while, it was within a certain perimeter. But when he got closer, we were forced to act.

—He got closer?

—He made a move toward us. He lunged.

—That's when you fired your gun?

—Yes. I did and the rest of the team did.

—How many bullets did the autopsy reveal had been fired into him?

—Three.

—But weren't you all shooting at him?

—No, only three of us fired our weapons.

—And did the three bullets stop him?

—Yes. He dropped to the ground.

—And then what?

—We approached him with caution, and when we saw that he had dropped the knife, we called the ambulance.

—And when did you know you'd killed him?

—A few hours later. We were at the hospital.

—You waited there at the hospital?

—Yes I did. There were at least six officers there. We did not want the young man to die.

—But you shot him.

—We shot him to subdue him.

—How close do you think he got to you?

—How do you mean?

—When he was stepping toward you, was he running?

—He moved very quickly.

—Was he running?

—He had begun to run, yes.

—And how far did he move toward you?

—We measured it at eight feet.

—Okay. So you said you had been twenty-five feet away from him. When you shot him, if he'd moved eight feet toward you, he was still seventeen feet away from you. Is that right?

—Yes.

—Okay, wait. Let me go over here. About as far away as I am from you now. Is this the distance?

—Yes. About.

—So he died about seventeen feet from you.

—Yes.

—How many times did you personally shoot him?

—Shoot or hit?

—Both.

—I shot three times and hit him once.

—Where did you hit him?

—Once in the neck.

—Is that where you were aiming?

—I was aiming at a figure moving quickly toward me. We're taught to aim into the largest part of the target. And that's the torso.

—You wanted to stop his forward motion.

—Yes.

—And you did stop it.

—Yes. Listen, I didn't enjoy it. I have never fired my weapon since that night. I'm not some cowboy. I know it doesn't diminish your pain, but it was traumatic for me, too. I would have preferred any other outcome.

—That's fine. But here's the thing: it seems like there were other possible outcomes. I just never understood the concept, the logistics of all this. There are twelve heavily armed men, and you're surrounding this small man with a knife. He has no criminal record, and the two things you know he's done wrong that night are he's danced on some tables at Denny's and pushed his mom against a wall. Then a couple hours later he's dead in his own backyard. This kind of thing happens once a week.

—Here it does?

—Somewhere it does. Last week they shot a guy in a wheelchair.

—An armed man threatens a group of police officers, there will be bad outcomes.

—The wheelchair guy had a length of pipe. Why not just leave him alone? With Don, you removed the mom from the house. Why not just let him sit around in the basement?

—Let an armed man accused of assault roam free?

—He's in his basement. He's not roaming anywhere.

—He was armed and probably psychotic. We have to presume he's dangerous.

—But you didn't really think he was dangerous.

—Of course we did.

—But you didn't. You worked in Marview. This is some confused young man with a steak knife. He had a college degree, no prior record.

—Lee Harvey Oswald didn't have a record, either.

—Good. Good one. But really, when the SWAT team showed up, did you ever think, Well, maybe this is a bit much for one guy in a basement?

—No. We have to prepare for the worst.

—Well, that's true in a way, isn't it? You guys prepare for the worst, even in Marview. Doesn't that seem insane? A bunch of little towns by the ocean have a SWAT team? In case we get attacked by some army of sea lions?

—We have a fire department, too, even when there hasn't been a fatal fire in twenty-two years.

—But firemen don't have guns. You know how many SWAT teams there are in the country now? Of course you don't. Fifty thousand. Every fucking suburb has a SWAT team. And it's not because there's been some sudden surge of hostage situations in Westchester and Orange County. It's because you fuckers like to get dressed up.

—That is incorrect.

—You love it. That's why you got into the line of work in the first place. The gear. The fucking Batman utility belt.

—You have no idea what you're talking about.

—I have every idea what I'm talking about because you killed my friend. Don't you ever say I don't know what the fuck I'm talking about. I know everything. I'm the moral man here. I'm the man of principle.

—

—You know I'm the moral man here.

—

—Tell me you understand that.

—I understand that you want me to believe it.

—You better believe it. Motherfucker, you better believe it. You're the one who fucked up. You have blood on your hands. You're soaked in the blood of an innocent. Do you realize that?

—It was an unfortunate incident.

—See, just those words indicate no respect for human life. An incident ends a human life? No, that's an apocalypse. The death of a young person for no reason is an apocalypse. It's not an incident. Don was not an incident. You understand that? Is a person an incident?

—No.

—Was my friend an incident?

—No.

—Did you participate in the apocalypse that ended my friend?

—

—Don't tempt me.

—Yes.

—And there was no other way to subdue him? A taser? Pepper spray? A big net? Rubber bullets? Think for a second.

—In hindsight, there might have been a different solution. But he was armed and seemed about to do something terrible. This is how it usually happens. A guy seems harmless and then has a night where things go down a rabbit hole and people get killed. Every murderer has to start somewhere, and we were determined to stop him from hurting anyone.

—Tell me this, though: the guy's in the basement. Do you think, if you had simply left him there at the house, someone would have been hurt? I mean, instead of the standoff, with you demanding him to come out and him getting increasingly agitated, what if you had just left? Take the mom, leave the house, leave him alone. What do you think would have happened?

—He could have gotten right back into a car and he could have done something far worse than he already had.

—But you could have followed him. You could follow him around all night.

—And then we have a high-speed chase.

—You really think this was destined for some disastrous result?

—He was in a fugue state. I think his behavior was getting increasingly bizarre and dangerous.

—So you're all standing around him, the small man with a steak knife. And you said he came toward you. I understand the need to protect yourself. But why shoot him in the head?

—I did not aim for his head.

—One of your colleagues did.

—My supposition is that that officer was aiming for his torso, too.

—But why not just shoot him in the leg?

—We're trained to stop the aggressor and remove the threat. The best way to do that is to shoot at the torso. The torso is the largest target, and shooting there is the best chance to stop his forward movement.

—But you shot him in the neck and someone else shot him in the eye.

—I missed. I aimed for his torso, but it all happened very quickly.

—So again, why not just shoot him in the leg? Even before he started moving toward you, why not just shoot him in the leg and call it a day? He'd be immobilized instantly.

—If I shoot at his leg and miss, he could very well come at me and stick the knife in my neck.

—You're serious. You were really worried that he'd hurt you.

—Of course I was. Have you heard of the twenty-one-foot rule?

—Tell me.

—The basic principle is that if a suspect is within twenty-one feet of an officer, and is holding an edged weapon like a knife, then that suspect presents a clear and present danger to the officer. And deadly force against him is justified.

—So if a man is holding a knife within twenty-one feet of a cop, the cop is justified in shooting him.

—If that suspect is threatening to use it, yes.

—Why twenty-one feet?

—That's the area the suspect could cover in a short amount of time—not enough time for the officer to escape or protect himself. This was based on research done by an officer in Salt Lake City.

—So tell me something. If I'm holding a knife, and you're twenty-two feet away, all you have to do is step one foot closer to me, and then you get to shoot me. Isn't that possible?

—No.

—Yes it is. By your interpretation, it's possible.

—The rule is a guideline for officers to know the distance within which the suspect could reasonably present a deadly threat.

—Does the suspect have to be moving toward you?

—Not necessarily. If he's threatening me with a knife, and he's within twenty-one feet, then I'm permitted to use deadly force.

—Oh shit.

—What?

—This is what I feared. I mean, I knew you could be one of those cops misinterpreting that rule, but I hoped you weren't. I wanted it to be more complicated.

—I'm not misinterpreting anything.

—But you are, you fucking asshole. The twenty-one-foot rule is . . . Do you really not know? You've got that look on your face that says you have no idea what I'm talking about but you think I might actually know something you don't.

—That isn't the look on my face. I'm tired, and now I'm getting angry.

—Stop. You have no idea. Let me describe what the twenty-one-foot rule actually is. The rule says that a suspect armed with a knife can cover twenty-one feet in the amount of time a cop can remove his gun from his holster, aim it and fire it. Do you understand?

—Yes. But I'm not sure that's correct.

—It's a guideline. If you're faced with a man armed with a knife, and you're within twenty-one feet, you should get your weapon out.

That's what the rule states. Just that you should have your weapon *unholstered* if an armed man is that close.

—I don't believe that's true.

—It is true. That's from the manual, you idiot.

—

—You have nothing to say?

—

—This is so fucked up. I think you shot my best friend because you and your buddies can't read. I think you shot my best friend in the neck and head because you thought there was some rule that allowed you to do it. Some rule that you were too lazy or stupid to actually look up and read. You hear that the rule says you have to shoot anyone with a knife if you're within twenty-one feet, and so you shoot a tiny guy holding a kitchen knife who poses no threat to anyone. Doesn't that seem fucked up to you? I'll answer for you. It is fucked up. And you're a fucking idiot. And you know what else? I don't think he was even moving. I know you say now that he was moving toward you, but I'm betting he wasn't. I know you got everyone to agree with you that he was moving, but I think he just turned toward you. The one autopsy said that the bullet entered his neck at an angle that indicated his head had just turned toward you. I think he turned toward you, and you freaked out and shot him. And you thought all this was acceptable because you were thinking of the twenty-one-foot rule, which you don't even fucking understand.

—You're mistaken on all your facts.

—I think you killed my friend because you can't read.

—Fuck you.

—Okay, maybe you can read. But think how silly it looks to the world that twelve cops in SWAT gear can't subdue one five foot seven man holding a kitchen knife. I mean, doesn't it make you feel a little embarrassed?

—No. These people don't understand the actual dangers.

—Because there aren't actual dangers in that situation.

—Do you know how long it takes for an agile person to cover that twenty-one feet? It's about a second and a half. In that time, if your friend had decided to stick that knife in my neck or my face, he would have done it.

—But you had your gun out.

—Yes, to prevent him from killing me.

—I'll tell you why you shot him. Because you were all gathered around him, and you assumed the logical end to that situation is your guns are fired and someone is dead. It doesn't seem right otherwise. Do you agree with that?

—No.

—That every story ends with the firing of a gun?

—No.

—That you should get your way, on your timetable?

—No.

—You were all yelling at him, saying drop the knife, do as we say, do it now, do it now. And he doesn't. He yells more. Your adrenaline boils. And you want it all to end. There must be an end, and it must come quickly. You can't wait. You can't back down. Your guns all drawn have failed to make him do what you want him to do, and that drives you all crazy. You think, You'll submit to our will.

—No.

—And you'll do it *now,* because we've already been here, what, ten minutes?

—

—That's enough time, right? Too much time. The narrative was departing from what you recognize as normal and true. Normal and true is that he submits or he dies on your timetable.

—No.

—Do you realize what a strange race of people we are? No one else expects to get their way like we do. Do you know the madness that this unleashes upon the world—that we expect to have our way every time we get some idea in our head? That twelve heavily armed men can surround one man with a steak knife and the outcome is a back-yard execution? Does that not indicate to you that we have work to do? That as a people we have improving to do?

—

—Well?

—Well what? Sure. We have improving to do. I'm chained to a post. *You* have improving to do. Your friend is dead. We have improving to do. This base is collapsing around us. We have improving to do. To know this—I can't see why this is helpful to you or anyone else. All this, and I don't think you've learned a thing.

—You're so wrong. God, I love how wrong you are.

BUILDING 55

—I just want you to know how wrong you are. How wrong you always are and always have been.

—That's fine, Thomas.

—It's all been necessary. I just solved the whole thing with Don. The cop confessed. I know everything.

—You brought a police officer out here?

—I can get anyone I want.

—Thomas, you must know that as your mother I care about your welfare. I don't want you killed. You must know that. I've been hearing helicopters and I have a bad feeling. And no matter our differences and issues, I want you to live and to heal.

—If that happens, you'll be no part of it. You didn't help at all. I had to do it myself. I brought the cop here and he was one of the ones who shot Don and now I know why.

—I hope you didn't harm him.

—I didn't.

—Those helicopters are getting closer, son.

—No. They came and went. And I hid the van in the old roller rink. I was meant to be here so the truth could come to me.

—I don't know why you've put such importance on Don's death *now.* You didn't even go to his funeral.

—That has nothing to do with anything.

—It's not like you were so close to him.

—He was my best friend.

—He was your best friend? You hadn't seen him in years.

—You don't know anything about it.

—But I do. You didn't even— Forget it.

—Say it, you horrible person.

—You *were* his best friend. But when you dropped him, how do you think a borderline guy like that . . .

—What?

—Nothing. Forget it.

—Say it again.

—Please. Forget it. I don't know what I'm saying.

—No, you don't.

BUILDING 60

—Do you know why you're here?

—No. Are you going to hurt me?

—No. But I need answers quick. There isn't much time left.

—Okay.

—You know the hospital where I found you—were you working there in 2012?

—Yes.

—What is your position there?

—I'm director of patient access.

—Good. Good. That's what I thought.

—How did you get me here?

—You remember getting into the elevator down to the garage?

—Yes. That was you.

—Yes. Then chloroform and a thirty-minute drive. You were the easiest, next to my mom. Now listen. Some of the people out here have been here for days, so this has to be quick. Do you remember Don Banh?

—No. Are you planning to hurt me?

—Let me spell his name, because I don't think you know how it was pronounced. B-A-N-H.

—Wait. The guy who was shot by the cops?

—Exactly.

—You knew him?

—I did. Do you remember me?

—You must be the guy who . . . The arson case.

—No. That wasn't me.

—What's your name?

—It doesn't matter. But I knew Don. Do you remember seeing me the night he was brought in?

—I don't know. Maybe. It was chaotic.

—But do you remember his mother?

—Yes.

—Do you remember denying her access to her son?

—No. I didn't deny her. Immediate family is always allowed to visit.

—Listen. I should have prefaced all of this by saying that you need to tell me everything and right away. I haven't harmed anyone so far, I haven't hurt the astronaut, but you provoke me when you lie. You're not behind that desk anymore. Now we have to tell the truth.

—I'm sorry.

—Are you ready now?

—Yes.

—So why didn't you let Don's mom see her son?

—The police told me it was a security risk.

—A security risk to let her see her dying son?

—Yes. But it wasn't my decision. There were a bunch of cops there, and they were talking to the head of the hospital, and I was just a girl at a desk.

—But you called security on her.

—I was told to call security, yes.

—And they removed Don's mother from the hospital.

—Yes.

—And I wasn't allowed to enter the building.

—Right.

—You remember me now?

—Yes.

—Thank you. I'm glad you do. When was Don's mom allowed to reenter the hospital?

—I don't know.

—Never. She was never allowed to reenter. She first saw her son when he was at the morgue. After the cops had done whatever they needed to do. They said he was only shot three times.

—That had nothing to do with me. But I can understand your frustration, and that it drove you to set the building on fire.

—I told you I didn't do that.

—Okay.

—Did you know that something untoward was happening in the hospital while you were preventing Don's mom and me and everyone else from entering?

—No. I didn't know anything at all. I was told that the patient was in critical condition and that we needed to limit the flow of people in the ER.

—But he wasn't in the ER.

—He started in the ER and then was moved to the critical care unit.

—And this unit had a half-dozen cops guarding it.

—I don't know about that. I work on the first floor, and the critical care unit is on the second floor.

—But what do you believe was happening up there?

—I don't know.

—What have you heard?

—Nothing.

—You lie. It's way too late to start lying.

—I heard that the police were worried about the whole thing.

—Explain that.

—They shot him a lot. I don't know. This is all just rumors.

—You know the paramedics.

—Yes. I knew them.

—You knew them for years, right?

—Yes.

—And what did they say? How many bullets did they say they saw in Don?

—I really don't know.

—Tell me what you heard.

—They said seventeen.

—I knew it. And all this time, you never told anyone that.

—I couldn't. And it wouldn't have helped anyone.

—Now do you know why I tried to burn down your hospital?

—Everyone assumed it was you.

—You prevented a mother from seeing her son. I was thrown out of the building, too. You sealed his records, everything. You were complicit in a horrific lie.

—What was I supposed to do? The guy was dying. He died within three hours of being admitted. There was no way to save him. It was incredible that he was alive at all when they brought him in. So nothing I could have done would have changed that outcome.

—But the police covered this up. They made it look like they exercised restraint, twelve cops and only three bullets. But we know it was more. We know they shot the fuck out of him—I heard at least ten times. And there were no repercussions for any of those cops.

—Listen. All of that is far beyond my purview.

—Your purview? Your purview? It's the Hippocratic oath, right? Does that involve the truth? You perpetrated a lie.

—I perpetrated nothing. And I'm not a doctor. I don't do that oath.

—You're disgusting.

—You're saying that because I heard some rumor from a paramedic I was somehow part of a big conspiracy? If you people wanted so badly to know what happened to the guy, his mom shouldn't have pushed so hard to have him cremated so soon. She cremated away all the evidence.

—Okay, this is why I tried to burn your hospital. First of all, my friend was dying inside your hospital and you wouldn't let me see him. Even when he was dead, you wouldn't let me see him, even when his mother gave her consent. Second, I stayed at the hospital for two days after he died, trying to get in and trying to help Don's mom get the hospital records and trying to talk to anyone who worked there. But you set your fucking security stooges on me every time, and one of them hit me in the head with a flashlight. Third, you fucking terrible person, Don's mom never asked for him to be cremated. She had no idea that was happening. They delivered a little box to her, with Don inside, and she had no idea what it was. It was some woman from the funeral home delivering this box to her. But she'd never ordered a cremation. Why would Mrs. Banh order a cremation? She wanted to find out what happened to him. She and I had been talking about it for two days, that once Don's body was released from the hospital we'd get an independent autopsy done. Then one day she shows up asking about his body, and you, and I swear to god it was you, you look on your computer and tell her he's been cremated.

—That was me.

—I knew it.

—I was reading a computer screen. I didn't order the cremation.

—But now are you putting this all together?

—Yes I am.

—Do you know the kinds of crimes you were part of now? First a man is shot for holding a steak knife in his backyard. Then we find out he's shot seventeen times. Then the cops won't let his mom see him. Then they burn his body without her permission.

—But she must have signed some form.

—She can't write in English! They signed it for her. They claimed that she asked for cremation verbally, and then she signed the form. And they thought they were so fucking clever, because they had a Vietnamese woman with limited English, so they could always claim it was some misunderstanding. And you know what else? Your fucking paramedic friends stole his watch.

—That's not a surprise.

—I bet it isn't. They steal all the time, don't they? They stole the dead guy's watch, probably for the same reason that the fuckers forged her signature on the cremation forms. They figured she couldn't advocate for herself. She's some helpless Vietnamese woman. And he's some kid with bullets in his body. If the paramedics take his watch, they can blame it on the cops, or vice versa. I mean, you guys have a top-to-bottom system of wrecking all hopes of humanity. You strip bare every vestige of dignity.

—I think you know that isn't true. The case with your friend was incredibly rare. And everyone was very scared.

—You threw a body in an oven to hide the evidence.

—I didn't do that. I had nothing to do with that.

—You were complicit.

—You think your friend is the only terrible thing that's ever happened in a hospital? I've worked in some good ones, but this hospital we're talking about is a mess of a place. There are disgusting things every day, and dignity is not an option. It's a river of human decay and mistakes made in haste. People die every day for reasons no one could ever justify. Too much of this drug, not enough of that. People come in with a cold and leave dead. And above it all we have a code of silence driven by fear.

—Oh God.

—We do more good than harm, for sure, but . . .

—You know, when your friend is transported from his backyard, full of bullets, to a hospital, you think he's going to a more honorable place. There are these places where we expect honor, and cleanliness, and a code of conduct. But every day there's another one of these places that slips from the list. It's a damned short list now, you know that?

—I do know that.

—I have an astronaut here who did everything he was told to do and it got him nowhere. He's one example. He reaches the pinnacle of his field and they give him a punch in the gut. On the other end of the scale there's Don, who wanted to be left alone, who was confused, and the price of being confused in this world is seventeen bullets in your own backyard.

BUILDING 53

—Congressman, did you do anything over there that surprised yourself?

—Sure. Wait. What time is it?

—Sorry to wake you up. There's just not much time left, and I have to get down to the beach soon, to see if this girl is there again.

—What's that? What girl?

—This woman who I like a great deal, sir. She's been walking on the beach with her dog, and yesterday we talked, and I know there's a reason she was there when I was there. But that's not why I wanted to talk to you. I was just spending some time with this lady, this other lady from the hospital I poured gasoline on, and at a certain point I knew I wasn't getting anywhere with her.

—Wait. You poured gasoline on—

—Not on the lady. On the hospital. It was minor. It was symbolic.

And she didn't know why I did what I did, because she's always been a perpetrator of the system, as opposed to a victim of it. I trust you know what I mean.

—Well, son, I understand you have a unique perspective on it. You say you took another person? This one a woman?

—She works at the hospital where my buddy was taken. They burned his body to hide the evidence. They shot him seventeen times and said it was three, so a few weeks later I poured some gasoline around the administrative part of the building, and I lit it.

—Anyone hurt?

—No sir.

—You intend to hurt anyone, son?

—No sir. But I had no other recourse. Or I didn't think I did. I wasn't about to sue them or some other useless thing. I wanted to make a point, and make it quickly. I needed to shove the dog's nose in the shit so they would make the connection.

—And you're saying you weren't caught?

—No. Some people thought it was me, but everything was all fucked up because of Don, and the cops didn't want to make it any worse, so they didn't pursue it.

—Did it solve anything for you, lighting that match?

—It felt pretty good in the moment. And when I saw the newspaper reports, and read about the administrative people all shaken up and scared, that felt good, too. The best thing was that some of their records were burned, and that felt like justice.

—It's not good that you went about it that way.

—They shot my friend.

—The hospital people didn't shoot your friend, son.

—Well, they helped kill him.

—I have a feeling he wasn't going to make it, what with seventeen bullets in him.

—You must have had moments like that, sir, where there's some human being that's acting like, well, shit. For some reason the hospital woman makes me madder than the cops who shot him. I mean, why is that? Two years later I still don't understand it.

—Killing feels more natural in some way. Killing is some kind of connection. It's a convoluted connection, but it is one. You know how when you're a kid, and you're wrestling around with some friend, there's always that moment when you think you could snap his arm or bite through his nose?

—Yes, yes! I know that.

—But what happened at the hospital is something else. It's not human. It's not primal. So we don't understand it. It's a more recent mutation. The things we all have, love and hate and passion, and the need to eat and yell and screw, these are things every human has. But there's this new mutation, this ability to stand between a human being and some small measure of justice and blame it on some regulation. To say that the form was filled out incorrectly.

—Yeah, yeah, what is that? That's the doom of us all.

—This is a new thing, son, and it's a frightening thing. It's something I saw every day in the VA. And if you think it's bad in some hospital, Christ, you wouldn't last a minute in Washington. Wait. You hear that?

—I do.

—I really think this is the end, son. That's at least three choppers, and they're getting closer. That's not good for you.

—They're going too fast. They'll pass.

—I think the clock's running out, kid. Now listen. There's no reason anyone has to be hurt. I've been thinking a lot about this and I have a plan for you.

—That's not necessary.

—I know it isn't. But listen. You've probably heard some pretty frequent helicopter activity out there, right?

—It's routine.

—It might. Might not. Now listen. I have some empathy for you. I think you are mixed up but I don't think you should die for it, okay?

—I won't. I have a plan.

—Well let me give you a better plan. This is the right plan. You ready?

—Sure.

—You trust your mother, correct?

—

—I'm going to hope that's an implicit yes.

—

—Good. So you leave this place with your mother. You drive to whatever town you want to drive to. Then you drop your mother off. Maybe you're headed to Mexico, in which case you give yourself seven or eight hours. You tell your mom that after eight hours she can call the police and let them know where we all are. That way you personally know we'll all be safe and more importantly, that she's safe, too, and not languishing here for days and days, right?

—

—See, you hadn't thought of that, I'm guessing. You probably had your own escape planned but not the rescue of your mom. Thomas, she probably needs care. How old is she?

—I don't know. Sixty-something.

—Okay. She is not suited for this kind of experience, do you understand me? So you need to remove her from this. You drive your mom to safety and then you give yourself enough time to make your way to and over the border. After that it's up to you.

—That's the most generous thing anyone's said to me. But what about Sara?

—Who's Sara?

—The woman on the beach.

—On what beach?

—I met a woman down there on the coast. And I think I already love her and there's some kind of destiny at play here. There's a glow around me, around everything I think about and everything I do, and I think it's brought her to me.

—Okay. Okay. Now listen. I don't know if you're going to fall in love here at Fort Ord with five people kidnapped and chained to posts. Okay?

—Six. And I disagree, Congressman. I really do. You should see her.

—I'm sure she's marvelous, son, but anything that keeps you here any longer guarantees your death, you understand me? She can't save you from a SWAT team.

—They won't get me. I have a plan.

—But my plan is better. My plan ensures that absolutely no one gets hurt. You go around and tell everyone you have chained up that they'll be found tomorrow, then you and your mom get out of here. This whole thing will be over and you'll be in Mexico living a new life. It's the only way. Anything else jeopardizes your life or hers.

—Congressman, you are such an honorable man. And I plan to model my life after you when I leave here. I plan to tell Sara about you, too. She wouldn't quite understand how we've been talking, but I'll figure out a way later on to explain our acquaintance.

—Son.

—Shit. I better get going. This is when she walks her dog. For now I have to make it look like a coincidence that I'm seeing her again but after today there won't be any need for any fakery or lies or anything like that. I'll bring my light down around her and I'll take her with me.

—Son.

—I've really enjoyed getting to know you, sir.

BUILDING 48

—I'm sorry. I'm so sorry, Sara. I wish I didn't have to bring you here this way. But you forced my hand.

—What is this?

—You look pretty out of it. I should have used less on you.

—Are you the guy from the beach? Where am I?

—Not far.

—Where's my dog?

—He's fine. I have him next door. I fed him.

—My head. I'm so dizzy.

—I'm really sorry. I should have used less on you for sure, given your size. That seems so obvious to me now. I'm so sorry. But again, I didn't want to do this at all.

—What is this?

—It's a shackle. It's loose. Don't pull on it.

—Why am I here?

—Just to talk.

—I don't understand.

—It's easier this way. I won't harm you. That's why I'm sitting all the way over here. It's not because I'm standoffish or anything.

—And what do you want from me?

—Do you remember when I held your hand?

—On the beach?

—Yes. Do you remember what you did?

—I didn't want to hold your hand.

—Right. And it got strange. So now I want to start over. I realize now that I was too forward down there. You had a right to pull away. It was too much too soon, and now I think we can slow down and talk this through.

—Talk what through?

—I have a proposal for you.

—Is this what you were talking about on the beach? The thing with the boat?

—It is, but I want to explain it better.

—I'm not going off in some boat with you.

—Let me explain.

—Please. Just let me go.

—Sara. Calm down. I'm calm. You should be calm. This is a normal enough situation. We're talking. I've stopped time so we can just talk. I won't harm you. I even gave you my pillow and sleeping bag. You can lie down if you want.

—I don't want to. I want to get out. I want to go home.

—Then just tell me why you wouldn't hold my hand.

—Hold your hand?

—When I tried you flinched and your eyes went cold.

—I didn't know you. You're some stranger on the beach and suddenly you take my hand and stare into my eyes like that? What did you want me to do?

—Well, this is where the proposal comes in. If you'll let me explain. Can I?

—I don't know.

—Okay. Thank you. First, I want to say that I like you a great deal. I think you're beautiful, and you're in many ways the manifestation of the ideals I've held for what a woman can be. Is it acceptable that I say that?

—Fine.

—You seem like an independent person. You're self-possessed. You can be alone. When I saw you from a distance even, I thought that you were someone like me. That you could walk alone on the shore and you sought out that kind of solitude. Is that accurate?

—Sure.

—And when we first met a few days ago, when I saw your face and heard your voice, your candor and your humor, the way you would smile while looking down, drawing arcs in the sand with your toe, I found you to be so charming and humble and warm. And do you remember when you asked me about the scar near my eye?

—Yes.

—No one's asked me about that in years. I can't remember the last time anyone cared. And that's when I took your hand. And I realize it was too sudden. It was too sudden to tell you about my plan, and the boat. I realize that. But I hope you can forgive me for being impetuous. It comes just from a sense of knowing what's right, and what should happen, and wanting to get started.

—And where are we going again?

—I can't tell you yet. Not until you agree. But I can guarantee you'll be safe, and I really know we'll be happy. I believe in the fulfillment of promises. And all this week there has been a confluence of forces that have brought me many truths and a semblance of progress and completion. Everything was making sense, and many things were coming together, and I thought the manifestation of all that was meeting you. I thought, and still think, that we were placed on that beach at the same time by a divine hand that intended us together.

—So we get on this boat and never come back?

—I don't know if we'll come back.

—And if I don't come?

—Then you don't come.

—You won't harm me.

—I would never harm you. I haven't harmed any of the others.

—There are others here like this? Chained up?

—Just six.

—Oh no.

—No one's hurt.

—Everyone's alive?

—Of course everyone's alive. I'm a moral man. Sara, you have to understand that this has been a certain week when I stopped time and asked questions. I'm just a normal man but I was able to do this and you have to admit that means some other force was at work, right? The first person I brought here was an astronaut. That means something's happening, right? Doesn't it mean that I'm touched in some way? That there's something like destiny at work?

—I have no idea.

—I would never believe in this kind of thing, either. Believe me. There's no way. But too many things have happened this week, and now I have to submit to all this.

—Submit to what?

—This design. This order of events. I think all of these opportunities were presented to me, in this order, so I could answer the questions I needed to answer, settle all that needed settling, and then start anew.

—I don't know what you're talking about.

—I know it's a lot. And there'll be plenty of time to explain later. But the thing is, I think this is the end. Time's running out.

—The helicopters. I knew something was up. They were looking for you.

—Maybe. Someone's coming soon, sure. With the congressman here it was only a matter of time. And once it gets dark, I figure this is it. We have just tonight to make it out of here. I have a way to get to the water, and I have a strong boat that will take us to the next place. And once we get there, we'll be free.

—But I don't want to go away somewhere.

—I know. I know you have a life here. And you don't know me very well. All I'm asking is that you take this small leap of faith. That you acknowledge the presence of something extraordinary here.

—This isn't extraordinary. It's debased. It's ugly.

—I told you: I didn't want it this way. I wanted to leave from the beach and that's why I took your hand. But that didn't happen, so this did. This is just a means, just a temporary thing. You can see my side of things, I hope. How else would I have a chance to tell you all this?

—I think you'll have to leave me behind.

—No. I don't think it's supposed to be that way. I think the way it's supposed to end is that you and I go together, away from here. I can't see how it could be any other way. I mean, I hadn't planned it this way; I thought I'd leave here alone. But then you were there, on the shore, alone every day, this ray of light. And I knew it couldn't be a coincidence. For once in my life there was logic, and an orderly procession of events, one leading to the next, every time I had an idea it worked out. I wanted the astronaut and found him. I wanted the congressman and I found him. And the cop— I mean, it couldn't be chance. It couldn't be random, especially given at the end of it all I found you. I didn't even seek you out. I didn't know I wanted you, but it's all so obvious now that it was all leading up to this, to us. Now we just have to complete it.

—Not we.

—Yes we.

—I think you're right that you have to leave soon. Otherwise you'll be caught, or more likely killed. But you have to leave without me. If you get away, write me a letter. We can start over that way.

—No. I don't want that.

—Please.

—No. I don't know how to convince you, but this has to be. It has to be now. Everything depends on it.

—Or what?

—Or I don't know.

—See, now you're scaring me.

—I thought you would understand.

—I don't understand. I'm not some part of your bizarre plan.

—It's not *my* plan. It's *the* plan.

—No. No. It's *your* plan. *You* did all this. Yourself. This is criminal behavior.

—You know that's not true. I'm a criminal because I held your hand?

—You're a criminal because you kidnapped me and brought me here and have me chained to whatever this is.

—It's a holdback for a cannon, I think. Every one of these buildings has one. They're incredibly strong.

—I don't care!

—But you stopped and you talked to me. You smiled a certain way.

—That beach is empty. It always is. You're the only person for miles. And I talked to you. Anything beyond that was your imagination.

—But why couldn't I expect that you would be interested in me?

—I don't know. I just wasn't. Now look at you. I would venture that I've shown pretty good judgment.

—But why else would I be there? Why would you be there? For a second it all made sense. This is the edge of the continent and we're there alone.

—Right. And even that first day, I saw something sharp and desperate in your eyes, and the fact that you currently have me chained up in an Army barracks answers your own question, doesn't it?

—There's no way you knew all that the first day.

—Did I know you were kidnapping people? No. You're right, it was beyond my imagining. But it seemed very much that your head had been screwed on one turn too tight.

—Wait. You're the second person to say that. The congressman said it, too.

—What congressman?

—The one I have a few buildings over.

—Please don't kill me.

—I won't. I haven't harmed anyone. Jesus, Sara, I didn't hurt the astronaut and I won't hurt you. The only one who says she's hurt is my mom but she's always bitching about something.

—I can't believe I'm here.

—Like I said, it could have been different. And it's not too late.

—Not too late for what? For you and me to fall in love?

—It doesn't have to be right away.

—No.

—You think my head's on too tight. What does that mean?

—Forget it.

—Please. You should just talk to me. I'm getting sort of desperate now. I don't want to threaten you but I had to do that with the others and I'm tired of the threats.

—You're tired of the threats.

—Just assume I can threaten you and it's better if you answer my questions. Why do you think my head's on one turn too tight? What does that mean?

—It means that they put a capable brain in your skull, and then when they put the cap on, they turned it one turn too tight. It makes for bad outcomes. I think of graduate students stuffing their colleagues into crevices, shooting professors, that kind of thing. People like you. Smart but nuts. One turn too tight.

—How is that my fault?

—How is it not your fault?

—You have no idea what they did to me.

—I really don't care what they did to you. I care what you did to *me*. What you've done to all the others.

—I haven't harmed anyone. The congressman's been here days and he's fine. He's great actually. He's the only one who ever came close to keeping a promise to me. I thought you'd be the one who would really do it, would do something real and pure. And just looking at you now I still think you could. I've learned so much that I know I would treat you well. You'd live an honorable life with me. I'd be true to you always.

—What the fuck are you talking about? You'd keep me in some dungeon probably.

—No. No. I wouldn't. That isn't something I would do.

—But is *this* something you would do?

—No. Not normally.

—So this behavior is anomalous.

—Sara. I was pushed to a certain point, so I picked up the astronaut. We talked for a while, and that went well, and it helped me a lot. I think it helped him, too. And that led to the congressman. And that led to my mom and Mr. Hansen and a couple of others and now you. And all these means are justified, because I met you.

—You said you had your mom out here?

—I do.

—So you're a family man.

—See, I like you so much. Someone so pretty with a sense of humor like that, with the ability to be alone. You must have gotten beautiful far past adolescence.

—

—Ah. I'm right. I know you. You know me. You were too tall too young. Or your hair wasn't blond. Your shoulders were too broad, you grew into your nose. Something like that. You found yourself alone a lot and you enjoyed it. You know I'm right. And you know I know you. We're not different. It's not too late to change your mind. I really think you'll like me.

—You know what? I think what you're heading for is one of those romances where the women write to the prisoners. I think you'll be going to prison, and some nice lonely lady will write to you. That's the destiny that I think is more logical here.

—Don't you think it's just inherently wrong that we could find ourselves alone on a beach, and we're the same age, and not so far apart in terms of body type and overall attractiveness, and still we don't end up together? That just seems wrong to me. We're in the middle of nowhere, at the edge of the continent, and still you won't have me.

—I'm sorry.

—Okay. I can see how you see all this. How you see me. But this is just the transitional stage. The pupal stage.

—And then what? You become a butterfly.

—No. Maybe. You know what I mean. We're trapped right now, both of us, but we can be free. Hold on. Hear that? It sounded like voices.

—You have to know you'll be caught. I don't want you dead.

—What's that supposed to mean?

—There's a part of me that thinks that's the proper and right result of all this. Somehow it seems the only way this can end. But maybe that's just because I read a lot of westerns.

—Why would a woman who walks the beach with a Labradoodle read westerns?

—For one thing, my people have been living out here since 1812. So when I read westerns, I feel like they're talking about me. The stories tell me how to live. And in those stories, people like you either get hanged or get shot. I've come to feel some comfort and satisfaction when that happens. I don't know if that's right, or if I'd feel right if that happened to you. But I'm pretty sure it will.

—I have a different plan.

—I bet you do. But I doubt it's such a good plan.

—No, it's a very good plan.

—You plan to kill yourself.

—No. But I am dying.

—You're not dying.

—Of course I'm dying.

—You didn't say anything about dying. What are you dying of?

—I'm dying. Leave it at that.

—Well, I'm sorry.

—It's okay.

—That explains a lot.

—Now you understand.

—If I had a limited time to live, I might do something radical.

—We can be together till I go.

—No.

—I find that heartless.

—It's not heartless.

—Especially given you're dying, too.

—I'm not dying.

—Of course you are. We all are.

—Oh Jesus. So you're not sick.

—We're declining, don't you see that? The second we reach adulthood we begin dying. There's nothing more obvious than that. You might live on and on till you're some doddering ghost but I'm thirty-four and Don's dead, and my father was forty-one when he left this world. This is my last chance.

—And what if it isn't?

—That would be horrific.

—Existing beyond thirty-four would be horrific.

—Existing, period—this is what drives men to irrational acts. You know this? I used to worry about something happening to me. That I'd be killed in my sleep by some intruder. That I'd be mugged, maimed, drafted, killed. And then the years went by and none of that happened, and what filled that void was far worse.

—I don't understand that.

—You don't know what it's like to be a man over thirty who's never had anything happen to him. You spend so many years trying to stay safe, stay alive, to avoid some unknown horror. Then you realize the horror is existence itself. The nothing-happening.

—You were bored.

—I wasn't *bored*. I was dying. I *am* dying. But this week was different. There was alignment and order and a coming-to.

—I don't know what to say to that.

—You know this land we're on? Twenty-eight thousand acres of buildings like this. Everything crumbling. They've left a thousand of these buildings rotting in the wind. No one has a clue what to do next. This vast military base and it's just decaying on the edge of the country. There's no plan for all this. No plan for anything. I found a yearbook for this place—it must have been from the late fifties. Company D, Third Battalion, Third Brigade. And on the cover of this yearbook is a picture of a soldier in a foxhole, watching something explode. They got right to the point: *Young men, come and blow things up*. It felt right. I felt at home.

—So join the Army.

—Sara, do you ride horses?

—When?

—Anytime.

—Yes.

—On the beach?

—Have I ridden a horse on the beach? Yes.

—Did they let you gallop?

—Did *who* let me gallop?

—Whoever makes the rules. I don't know.

—Sure. I gallop.

—You gallop on a horse on the beach?

—Sure.

—Was it good?

—Yes, it's good.

—It always looked good. Is it hard?

—It takes some practice.

—You learned it yourself?

—I took lessons when I was a kid.

—And they let you gallop then?

—When I was young?

—When you were young.

—Yes.

—I've been on horses but we always have to walk around. It's so meaningless. The horse hates it, and it's so slow, and we just walk around and everyone sweats. And each time I asked if we could gallop and they always said no, no. Insurance liability, you'll get hurt, blah blah. But there's no point in walking around on top of a horse. It gives no pleasure to anyone. The only point is galloping.

—But it takes a while. A lot of practice.

—How long?

—Till they let you gallop? A while.

—See, no one told me that. If someone had explained the steps, I would have had a chance.

—No offense, Thomas, but my guess is you're inclined toward shortcuts.

—Because I want to get on a horse and gallop?

—Yes. You see something and you want it. But you don't want to do any of the steps to get there.

—And whose fault is that?

—I'm guessing someone else's?

—No one told me the steps.

—The steps? No one told you to work hard?

—I had no role models.

—Oh Jesus Christ. Stop.

—So you're saying it's about hard work and follow-through and patience and all that shit.

—I guess that's what I'm saying.

—And what good does that do? You know the astronaut I have over there? Eighteen years of work and preparation and doing all the shit he's supposed to do, and where is he?

—He's shackled to a post, I'm guessing.

—Okay, but in general, where is he? He's supposed to be on the Shuttle, but he's still picking his ass, waiting to maybe ride on a Russian rocket to some hamster wheel in space. All the things he worked for no longer exist.

—But it would all be better if you could gallop.

—It could be.

—And where would you go?

—I don't know.

—Thomas, we all get what we work for. Maybe there's some variation, but still. I worked nine years to be a vet and wanted to work in Boulder. I'm a vet and I work in Monterey. You see what I'm saying? Your friend wanted to be an astronaut and he's an astronaut. Maybe he's going on a different spaceship. So what?

—If you knew anything about the Shuttle you wouldn't say that. There's a big difference between a reusable spacecraft that can land and maneuver, and a stupid fuck-all stationary space kite like the ISS. Sara, I just want to get something I want. I don't think I've ever gotten any significant thing I wanted. You have no idea how weird it is to envision things and have them come to nothing. No vision has ever come true, no promise has ever been kept. But then there was you,

and you were the promise that would obliterate all the disappoint-
ments of the past. Everything about you insisted on it. Your color,
your hair, the way light projects from every part of you. You were
the sun that would burn away all the putrid broken promises of the
world.

—I wasn't that.

—I know that now.

—The helicopters are getting louder. They found you.

—They found us. You know, I really don't want to be caught.

—Thomas, please let me live.

—I'm not going to hurt you. Wow, they are really getting close.

—Okay. Let's go.

—What? What do you mean?

—I'm ready. Let's go. I want to go with you.

—No you don't.

—I do. I've been sitting here thinking, and even while I was
denying it to you I was realizing that you're right. These can't all be
coincidences. An astronaut, a congressman, your mom, me. It all has
to mean something.

—It does, right?

—It does. If I say I'll go with you, you'll unlock me?

—Of course. I'll have to have us handcuffed together, though.

—And then what?

—We run to the shore and to the boat.

—What about the others?

—They'll be fine.

—Are there really others?

—Of course. Six of them.

—Will you let me see them?

—No. Why?

—If I'm going off with you, I need to make sure you haven't harmed anyone.

—You don't trust me. And there's no time.

—I do trust you.

—We don't have time to go visiting everyone. And you don't want to meet my mom. She wouldn't believe we were together anyway.

—So we don't visit your mom. Just let me see the astronaut.

—No. He's a phony. I already said good-bye to him and everyone else. I'll let you see the congressman.

—Okay. Let's go.

—So I unlock you and we go and see the congressman and you come with me?

—If we get away.

—What do you mean, *if* we get away?

—They're so close. We'll have to hurry. And you'll have to let me run free, too. If we're handcuffed we'll be too slow.

—But then we might get separated.

—No we won't.

—Oh no. You're trying to get away.

—No.

—From me!

—No, I just think we'll be faster that way.

—I don't think you believe in me.

—I do. Of course I do.

—I don't think you believe in any of this.

—I do. I do. But we should go. I want to go together.

—Oh god.

—What?

—You're trying to trick me.

—I'm not.

—All this time I've been so direct with you. I've told you what I believed should happen. I've told you what I want and what would be best for both of us. I've offered you the chance to be part of something like destiny, and you're just trying to slither out of it.

—Thomas. I just think we should go.

—I'm not going with you. Oh shit, you just murdered me.

—No. Thomas.

—You're just like Kev. You seem like these paragons of virtue and heroism but in the end you just want to stay alive. You don't want to be part of anything extraordinary.

—Don't hurt me now.

—I'm not going to hurt you.

—Promise me.

—Forget it. I'm leaving.

—And I'll be safe?

—To what end?

—To keep living.

—That's my point. That's not enough.

BUILDING 53

—Congressman?

—They're all over the place, kid. Don't you see? Stay away from the windows.

—Are you okay?

—I'm fine. But you're as good as dead. Stay low, and close to me.

—That's okay. I can stay here.

—At least stay low. Stay alive.

—You know, you're my only friend. My only living friend.

—What about the astronaut?

—He's no astronaut. Not my kind of astronaut. And every other light has gone out. You see how dark it is out there? But I think you and I are the same. You're the man I'd like to be.

—Missing two limbs.

—It doesn't matter. You're the only person I've ever known who means what they say.

—Okay.

—You're like a father to me.

—Thomas, please keep your head away from the windows.

—Sorry. Do you know that no man has ever given me advice like you have? Listened to me like you have?

—That can't be. At your age? How old did you say you are again, son?

—Thirty-four.

—Christ on a cracker.

—There are millions more like me, too. Everyone I know is like me.

—I thought you were twenty-five. God help us.

—Like I said the other day, if there were some sort of plan for men like me, I think we could do a lot of good.

—You talking about your canal again?

—A canal, a spaceship. A moon colony. Maybe just a bridge. I don't know. But the walking around, sitting, eating at tables . . . It doesn't work. We need something else.

—What do you want to build? The world's already built.

—So I just walk around in an already-built world? That's a joke.

—That's the joke you live in.

—But that's a perfect inversion of why I exist. I'm the guy who you send to dynamite the mountain to make way for the railroad. I'm the guy who gallops through the West with a load of dynamite to blow the fucking mountain.

—To clear a path.

—For the railroad. Right. I was supposed to be that guy.

—It's too late for that. Two hundred years too late.

—I showed up two hundred years late for the life I was supposed to live.

—I hear you, son. I truly do.

—Do you? Does anyone else?

—I don't know.

—What they don't realize is that we need something grand, something to be part of.

—And the Shuttle was that for you?

—I don't know. Maybe the Shuttle was some dumb fucking space glider. But now it's dead and Don's dead and Kev is chained to a post. Fuck it. And you know what's really pathetic about Don being shot by twelve cops in his backyard? It meant nothing to no one. He was no martyr, he died for no ideals. And the only thing worse than the silencing of a martyr, a real martyr—someone with dangerous ideas—is silencing someone who has nothing at all to say. Don wasn't opposed to anything but himself.

—I'm sorry about all this, Thomas.

—But this'll keep happening. You know that, right? If you don't have something grand for men like us to be part of, we will take apart all the little things. Neighborhood by neighborhood. Building by building. Family by family. Don't you see that?

—I believe I do.

—Who says we don't want to be inspired? We fucking want to be inspired! What the fuck is wrong with us wanting to be inspired?

Everyone acts like it's some crazy idea, some outrageous ungrant-able request. Don't we deserve grand human projects that give us meaning?

—Thomas, there's a light under the door. I believe they're here.

—Of course they are. You can tell them you're here. I'm done.

—You want me to call out?

—Go ahead.

—We're in here! Everyone's safe.

—God, that sounds really horrible, doesn't it? Nothing in the world sounds worse than that, to be here and safe. Say it again. I don't think they heard you.

—We're in here and we're safe.

—Jesus Christ. That is the saddest thing I ever heard.

ou Vidas and

Daniel Gumbiner,

rd, Andi

an, Gabrielle

ndrew Wylie and

opf and Vintage.

Enid Baxter Ryce

BOOKS BY THIS AUTHOR

A NOTE ABOUT THE AUTHOR

Dave Eggers is the author of nine books, including most recently *The Circle* and *A Hologram for the King,* which was a finalist for the 2012 National Book Award. He is the founder of McSweeney's, an independent publishing company based in San Francisco that produces books, a quarterly journal of new writing (*McSweeney's Quarterly Concern*), and a monthly magazine (*The Believer*). McSweeney's also publishes Voice of Witness, a nonprofit book series that uses oral history to illuminate human rights crises around the world. Eggers is the cofounder of 826 National, a network of eight tutoring centers around the country, and ScholarMatch, a nonprofit organization designed to connect students with resources, schools, and donors to make college possible. He lives in Northern California with his family.

www.mcsweeneys.net
www.voiceofwitness.org
www.826national.org
www.scholarmatch.org
www.valentinoachakdeng.org